Winfield Scott

Memoirs of Lieut.-General Scott, LL. D

Volume II.

Winfield Scott

Memoirs of Lieut.-General Scott, LL. D
Volume II.

ISBN/EAN: 9783337001513

Printed in Europe, USA, Canada, Australia, Japan

Cover: Foto ©Raphael Reischuk / pixelio.de

More available books at **www.hansebooks.com**

MEMOIRS

OF

LIEUT.-GENERAL SCOTT, LL.D.

Written by Himself.

IN TWO VOLUMES.

VOLUME II.

NEW YORK:

SHELDON & COMPANY, PUBLISHERS,
335 BROADWAY,
1864.

CONTENTS OF VOL. II.

Contents.

CHAPTER XXIX.

CHAPTER XXX.

CHAPTER XXXI.

CHAPTER XXXII.

CHAPTER XXXIII.

CHAPTER XXXIV.

CHAPTER XXXV.

CHAPTER XXXVI.

CHAPTER XXIII.

IT has been said that the autobiographer had intended to accompany the emigration farther west than the Ohio, to help it through any unforeseen difficulties on the route; but short of that point he received despatches from Washington telling him that the *Canadian patriots* (taking advantage of his absence in the South) had, in great numbers, reorganized their secret lodges all along the frontiers, and would renew their attempts to break into the Canadas on the return of frost, and he was directed to hasten thither, arranging with the Governors of Kentucky and Ohio, in route, the supply of such uninfected volunteers as might be needed to maintain the obligations of neutrality toward Great Britain.

Accompanied by Captain Robert Anderson, Scott rapidly visited Frankfort and Columbus; made contingent arrangements for volunteers that might be wanted, and also with the United States' District Attorney of Ohio for the assistance of his deputies and marshals in the arrest of leading offenders. Several of these, accompanied by a deputy marshal, he pursued for days. Though he lost not a moment on the route, he arrived but in time at Cleveland, Sandusky, and Detroit, respectively, to stop and disperse multitudes of frenzied citizens, by the means used in the previous winter, and thence proceeded down the frontiers *via* the places named, to Buffalo, Oswego, Sackett's Harbor, Ogdensburg, and Plattsburg, to the northern frontier of Vermont—meeting like assemblages and successes everywhere.

At the point farthest east he heard of the forward movement of the State of Maine on the Aroostook question, and fortunately was sufficiently out of work to hasten to Washington for instructions on this new difficulty—one entirely independent of Canadian patriots and sympathizers.

The autobiographer reported himself in person to the Secretary of War, without having been in a recumbent position in eighty hours. Every branch of the Government felt alarmed at the imminent hazard of a formidable war—but little having been done in a twenty-four years' peace to meet such exigency.

Though the moments were precious, Scott was detained several days to aid by explanations and arguments the passage of two bills—one to authorize the President to call out militia for six, instead of three months, and to accept fifty thousand volunteers; the other to place to his credit ten millions of dollars *extra.* For that purpose, he (Scott) was taken into conference with the chairmen of the committees on foreign and military affairs, of both Houses of Congress, and he may add, excusably, he hopes, that but for his expositions, and the known fact that the whole management of the difficulty in question would devolve on him, the bills would not have become laws; for, besides a hesitancy in the House of Representatives, a decided majority of the Senate was opposed to the Administration.

In taking leave of Mr. Van Buren and Mr. Secretary Poinsett, in order that there might be no " untoward" mistake, Scott respectfully said: "Mr. President, if you want *war*, I need only look on in silence. The Maine people will make it for you fast and hot enough. I know them; but if *peace* be your wish, I can give no assurance of success. The difficulties in its way will be formidable." "Peace with honor," was the reply; and that being Scott's own wish—looking to the great interests of the country—he went forward with a hearty good will.

Always accompanied by the gallant Captain Robert Anderson, and now rejoined by Lieutenant Keyes, Aide-de-Camp, the autobiographer, with *carte blanche*, hastened toward Maine — stopping in Boston long enough to arrange a contingent call for militia and volunteers with the patriotic and most accomplished Governor—Edward Everett—who, at the presentation to the executive council overwhelmed the sleepless general by this address:

"GENERAL:

"I take great pleasure in introducing you to the members of the Executive Council of Massachusetts; I need not say that you are already known to them by reputation. They are familiar with your fame as it is recorded in some of the arduous and honorable fields of the country's struggles. We rejoice in meeting you on this occasion, charged as you are with a most momentous mission by the President of the United States. We are sure you are intrusted with a duty most grateful to your feelings—that of averting an appeal to arms. We place unlimited reliance on your spirit, energy, and discretion. Should you unhappily fail in your efforts, under the instructions of the President, to restore harmony, we know that you are equally prepared for a still more responsible duty. Should that event unhappily occur, I beg you to depend on the firm support of the Commonwealth of Massachusetts."

The general replied most respectfully, and concluded with assuring the Governor and council that the Executive of the United States had full reliance on the patriotism and public spirit of Massachusetts, to meet any emergency which might arise.

From that scene Scott was next taken to the popular branch of the legislature, where he was also handsomely received — another life-long, valued friend, Robert C. Winthrop, subsequently distinguished in both Houses of Congress, in the chair.

Arriving at Portland, Scott met his first difficulty. The whole population, it seemed, had turned out to greet him. All being in favor of war, or the peaceful possession of the Aroostook, the "disputed territory," all looked to him to conquer that possession at once, as they had become tired of diplomacy, parleys, and delays. Many of his old soldiers of the last war with Great Britain were in the crowd; and although no man is a hero in the estimation of his *valet de chambre*, the feeling is quite otherwise with a commander's old brothers in arms. These now exaggerated Scott into the greatest man-slayer extant;—one who had killed off, in the Canadas, more men than Great Britain had there in that war.

Loud calls were made for a speech, *a speech!* But, too young in diplomacy to have acquired the art of using language to conceal his thoughts, the missionary of peace took refuge in silence, being, really, much oppressed with a cold and hoarseness. The word *peace* he had to hold *in petto*, to be suggested in the gentlest and most persuasive accents to the hostile ears of the Governor and his council at Augusta, the capital of Maine.

Scott found a bad temper prevailing at Augusta.

The legislature was in session, and the Democrats dominant in every branch of the Government.

In the legislature the weight of talent and information, however, was with the Whig minority. Hence they were much feared; for, having recently been in power, the least error on the side of the Democrats, might again give them the State. The popular cry being for war, the Whigs were unwilling to abandon that hobby-horse entirely; but the Democrats were the first in the saddle and rode furiously.

The State of Maine and the Province of New Brunswick were fast approaching actual hostilities, and if Scott had been a few days later in coming upon the scene, the troops of the two countries would have arrived, and crossed bayonets on the disputed territory —a strip of land lying between acknowledged boundaries, without any immediate value except for the fine ship-timber in which it abounded. The cutting of these venerable trees by British subjects led Maine to send a land agent, with a *posse*, to drive off the trespassers. The agent was seized and imprisoned, for a time, in the Province. Much angry correspondence ensued between the two Governors, followed by ominous silence and war preparation.

15

Scott soon perceived that the only hope of pacification depended on his persuading the local belligerents to stand off the territory in question for a time, and to remit the whole question in issue to the two paramount Governments at Washington and London, from which it had been improperly wrested, by the impatience of Maine at the dilatoriness of American diplomacy.

He took up his quarters at the same house, in Augusta, with His Excellency and other leading Democrats, and sat in the midst of them three times a day at the same public table. By degrees he won their confidence. He was known to them as the representative, in the special matter, of their friends of the same party at Washington.

The intrinsic difficulties to be dealt with in the mission were much aggravated by a new element just thrown in by federal authority and published at the time in all the papers, viz. :

"MEMORANDUM.

" Her Majesty's authorities consider it to have been understood and agreed upon by the two Governments, that the territory in dispute between Great Britain and the United States, on the northeastern frontier, should remain exclusively under British jurisdiction until the final settlement of the boundary question.

" The United States' Government have not understood the above agreement in the same sense, but consider, on the contrary, that there has been no agreement whatever for the exercise, by Great Britain, of exclusive jurisdiction over the disputed territory, or any portion thereof, but a mutual understanding that, pending the negotiation, the jurisdiction then exercised by either party, over small portions of the territory in dispute, should not be enlarged, but be continued merely for the preservation of local tranquillity and the public property, both forbearing as far as practicable to exert any authority, and, when any should be exercised by either, placing upon the conduct of each other the most favorable construction.

" A complete understanding upon the question, thus placed at issue, of present jurisdiction, can only be arrived at by friendly discussion between the Governments of the United States and Great Britain; and, as it is confidently hoped that there will be an early settlement of the question, this subordinate point of difference can be of but little moment.

"In the mean time, the Governor of the Province of New Brunswick and the Government of the State of Maine, will act as follows: Her Majesty's officers will not seek to expel, by military force, the armed party which has been sent by Maine into the district bordering on the Aroostook River; but the Government of Maine will, voluntarily, and without needless delay, withdraw beyond the bounds of the disputed territory any armed force now within them; and if future necessity should arise for dispersing notorious trespassers, or protecting public property from depredation by armed force, the operation shall be conducted by concert, jointly or separately, according to agreements between the Governments of Maine and New Brunswick.

"The civil officers in the service respectively of New Brunswick and Maine, who have been taken into custody by the opposite parties, shall be released.

"Nothing in this memorandum shall be construed to fortify or to weaken, in any respect whatever, the claim of either party to the ultimate possession of the disputed territory.

"The Minister Plenipotentiary of Her Britannic Majesty having no specific authority to make any arrangement on the subject, the undersigned can only recommend, as they now earnestly do, to the Governments of New Brunswick and Maine, to regulate their future proceedings according to the terms herein set forth, until the final settlement of the territorial dispute, or until the Governments of the United States and Great Britain shall come to some definite conclusion on the subordinate point upon which they are now at issue.

" JOHN FORSYTH, *Secretary of State
of the United States of North America.*
" H. S. Fox, *H. B. M. Envoy
Extraordinary and Minister Plenipotentiary.*

" WASHINGTON, *February* 27, 1839."

This *memorandum* gave great offence to the authorities and people of Maine. They were required to withdraw their forces from the territory in dispute simply on the promise that British officers would not *seek to expel them by force!*—without any reciprocal obligation;—the other party being left free to remain; to fortify themselves; to continue their depredations, undisturbed, and for an indefinite time! This bungle Scott had first to adjust between Democratic authorities

—State and Federal—he being himself a Whig! It was no easy thing to find a solvent for such knarled perplexities, foreign and domestic. Fortunately accidental circumstances in his history supplied the *desideratum.*

The Governor of the Province, New Brunswick, was, at the time, the distinguished Lieutenant-General, Sir John Harvey, of the British army, the same who in the campaign of 1813 was adjutant-general in Upper Canada with the rank of lieutenant-colonel. (See above, p. 99 and note.)

The report of Colonel Harvey's kindness to such American officers and men as fell into the hands of the enemy, made him an object of respect and kindness throughout our ranks. Harvey and Scott being leaders, and always in front, exchanged salutes several times on the field, and once, when out reconnoitring, Scott's escort cut off the Englishman from his party. A soldier, taking a deadly aim, would, certainly, have finished a gallant career, if Scott had not knocked up the rifle—saying, *Don't kill our prisoner!* But though a prisoner for a moment, Harvey, by a sudden movement, spurred his charger and escaped into a thicket, unhurt, notwithstanding the many rifle balls hastily thrown after him. This was the second time that he had escaped from captivity, and Scott now gave strict orders never to spare again an enemy so active and dangerous.

It so happened that in leaving the Cherokee country, the *major*-general received a friendly letter from the *lieutenant*-general, which, from the want of time, remained unanswered when the former arrived at Augusta.

The reply to that letter, semi-official, was followed by a rapid interchange of like communications, the Governor of Maine reading all that was written by the correspondents. By degrees Scott won over to his pacific views the dominant party—only that it hesitated lest the Whigs should shift about, agitate against any compromise and thereby regain the State. This apprehension was mentioned to Scott by the Governor, in the presence of the aged treasurer, an honest man, but a bigot in politics. Scott, who had not approached the Whigs in the Legislature, who, indeed, had shunned him as a Democrat;—nor had he expressed a party sentiment to anybody after his leaving Washington—now. asked permission of Governor Fairfield to speak to his leading opponents in that body—adding that he himself being a Whig, might bring them out, openly, in support of pacific measures. At this declaration of party bias, the good old treasurer was thrown into a most ludicrous attitude of surprise and consternation, which caused his Excellency, though himself, at first, a little startled, to laugh most heartily. This burst of good humor, in which the treasurer eventually joined, was a positive gain in the right direction. (All the details of this negotiation cannot yet be given. There was, however, no bribery.)

To bring those leading Whigs and Scott together required dexterous management; for if that had happened without the presence of leading Democrats, a suspicion of foul play would have been excited. Scott, therefore, induced Senator Evans, just from Washington, to invite them, the Governor and several State Councillors to sup with him at Gardiner, a little below Augusta. The envoy took charge of his Democratic friends in a government sleigh. All the topics he intended to urge upon the Whig leaders were given and discussed in the vehicle. The night was brilliant, and so was the entertainment. Mr. Evans—a distinguished Whig, as everybody knew — placed his Democratic guests at his end of the table, and Scott, with the

Whigs around him, at the other. The latter were sulky, and Scott's blandishments, in doing the honors of his position, failed to open the way to the main business of the evening—next to the supper—when, on a beckon, the master of the feast came to the rescue, and whispered to the Whigs (capital fellows!) that the representative of President Van Buren, near them, was as good a Whig as the best of them! Another ludicrous surprise! Compliments and cordiality ensued at once, and viands and business were discussed together to the content of all parties. The Governor understood the object of the Senator's whispers, and plainly saw that Scott had succeeded. A feast is a great peacemaker—worth more than all the usual arts of diplomacy. Scott had also, from the first, received good assistance from the Honorable Albert Smith, of Portland, afterward a member of Congress, who, happening to be in Augusta, gave him the temper and bias of many particular Democrats whom it was necessary to conciliate.

The work was done. Virtually nothing remained, but the synthetic process of gathering up all the particular results into one general act of amnesty and good will. Sir John Harvey was of a too elevated character

15*

to be fastidious about non-essentials. On being sounded, he had concurred at once with Scott on all essentials, and Governor Fairfield and council having no longer anything to fear from perversity on the part of the Whigs, now sent in a message, March 12, to the Legislature, of which this is an extract:

"What then shall be done? The people of the State surely are not desirous of hurrying the two nations into a war. Such an event is anxiously to be avoided, if it can be without dishonor. We owe too much to the Union, to ourselves, and, above all, to the spirit and principles of Christianity, to bring about a conflict of arms with a people having with us a common origin, speaking a common language, and bound to us by so many ties of common interest, without the most inexorable necessity. Under these circumstances I would recommend that, when we are fully satisfied, either by the declarations of the Lieutenant-Governor of New Brunswick, or otherwise, that he has abandoned all idea of occupying the disputed territory with a military force, and of attempting an expulsion of our party, that then the Governor be authorized to withdraw our military force, leaving the land-agent with a posse, armed or unarmed, as the case may require, sufficient to carry into effect your original design—that of driving out or arresting the trespassers, and preserving and protecting the timber from their depredations."

The Legislature, on the 20th of the same month, passed an act in accordance with the message, and the next day Scott despatched by his line of couriers, to meet Sir John's line at the border, the following papers:

From the Augusta (Me.) Journal, March 26, 1839.

" *The War Ended.—Important Correspondence.*

HEADQUARTERS, EASTERN DIVISION
U. S. ARMY, AUGUSTA, ME.,
March 21, 1839.

" ' The undersigned, a Major-General in the Army of the United States, being specially charged with maintaining the peace and safety of their entire northern and eastern frontiers, having cause to apprehend a collision of arms between the proximate forces of New Brunswick and the State of Maine on the *disputed territory*, which is claimed by both, has the honor, in the sincere desire of the United States to preserve the relations of peace and amity with Great Britain—relations which might be much endangered by such untoward collision—to invite from his Excellency Major-General Sir John Harvey, Lieutenant-Governor, etc., etc., a general declaration to this effect:

" ' That it is not the intention of the Lieutenant-Governor of Her Britannic Majesty's Province of New Brunswick, under the expected renewal of negotiations between the cabinets of London and Washington on the subject of the said disputed territory, without renewed instructions to that effect from his Government, to seek to take military possession of that territory, or to seek, by military force, to expel therefrom the armed civil *posse* or the troops of Maine.

" ' Should the undersigned have the honor to be favored with such declaration or assurance, to be by him communicated to his Excellency the Governor of the State of Maine, the undersigned does not in the least doubt that he would be immediately and fully authorized by the Governor of Maine to communicate to his Excellency, the Lieutenant-Governor of New Brunswick, a corresponding pacific declaration to this effect:

" ' That, in the hope of a speedy and satisfactory settlement, by negotiation, between the Governments of the United States and Great Britain, of the principal or boundary question between the State of Maine and the Province of New Brunswick, it is not the intention of the Governor of Maine, without renewed instructions from the Legislature of the State, to attempt to disturb by arms the said Province in the possession of the Madawaska settlements, or to attempt to interrupt the usual communications between that Province and Her Majesty's Upper Provinces; and that he is willing, in the mean time, to leave the questions of possession and jurisdiction as they at present stand—that is, Great Britain holding, in fact, possession of a part of the said territory, and the Government of Maine denying her right to such possession; and the State of Maine holding, in fact, possession of another portion of the same territory, to which her right is denied by Great Britain.

" ' With this understanding, the Governor of Maine will, without unnecessary delay, withdraw the military force of the State from the said disputed territory— leaving only, under a land agent, a small civil *posse*, armed or unarmed, to protect the timber recently cut, and to prevent future depredations.

"'Reciprocal assurances of the foregoing friendly character having been, through the undersigned, interchanged, all danger of collision between the immediate parties to the controversy will be at once removed, and time allowed the United States and Great Britain to settle amicably the great question of limits.

"'The undersigned has much pleasure in renewing to his Excellency Major-General Sir John Harvey, the assurances of his ancient high consideration and respect.

"'WINFIELD SCOTT.'

"To a copy of the foregoing. Sir John Harvey annexed the following:

"'The undersigned, Major-General Sir John Harvey, Lieutenant-Governor of Her Britannic Majesty's Province of New Brunswick, having received a proposition from Major-General Winfield Scott, of the United States' Army, of which the foregoing is a copy, hereby, on his part, signifies his concurrence and acquiescence therein.

"'Sir John Harvey renews with great pleasure to

Major-General Scott the assurances of his warmest personal consideration, regard, and respect.

" 'J. HARVEY.

" 'GOVERNMENT HOUSE, FREDERICTON,   }
   NEW BRUNSWICK, *March* 23, 1839.' }

" To a paper containing the note of General Scott,
and the acceptance of Sir John Harvey, Governor Fairfield annexed his acceptance in these words:

" 'EXECUTIVE DEPARTMENT,   }
   AUGUSTA, *March* 25, 1839. }

" ' The undersigned, Governor of Maine, in consideration of the foregoing, the exigency for calling out
the troops of Maine having ceased, has no hesitation in
signifying his entire acquiescence in the proposition of
Major-General Scott.

" ' The undersigned has the honor to tender to
Major-General Scott the assurance of his high respect
and esteem.

" 'JOHN FAIRFIELD.'

" We learn that General Scott has interchanged the
acceptances of the Governor and Lieutenant-Governor,

and also that Governor Fairfield immediately issued orders recalling the troops of Maine, and for organizing the civil *posse* that is to be continued, for the time, in *the disputed territory.* The troops in this town will also be immediately discharged."

With Sir John's acceptance came this letter:

" MY DEAR GENERAL SCOTT:

" Upon my return from closing the session of the Provincial Legislature, I was gratified by the receipt of your very satisfactory communication of the 21st instant. My reliance upon *you*, my dear General, has led me to give my willing assent to the proposition which you have made yourself the very acceptable means of conveying to me; and I trust that as far as the Province and the State respectively are concerned, an end will be put by it to all border disputes, and a way opened to an amicable adjustment of the national question involved. I shall hope to receive the confirmation of this arrangement on the part of the State of Maine at as early a period as may be practicable."

Dr. W. E. Channing, a leading philanthropist

scholar, orator, and divine, of his day, in the preface to his *Lecture on War* (1839), devoted two paragraphs to the honor of the autobiographer's peace labors, in these words:

" To this distinguished man belongs the rare honor of uniting with military energy and daring, the spirit of a philanthropist. His exploits in the field, which placed him in the first rank of our soldiers, have been obscured by the purer and more lasting glory of a pacificator, and of a friend of mankind. In the whole history of the intercourse of civilized with barbarous or half-civilized communities, we doubt whether a brighter page can be found than that which records his agency in the removal of the Cherokees. As far as the wrongs done to this race can be atoned for, General Scott has made the expiation.

" In his recent mission to the disturbed borders of our country, he has succeeded, not so much by policy as by the nobleness and generosity of his character, by moral influences, by the earnest conviction with which he has enforced on all with whom he has had to do, the obligations of patriotism, justice, humanity, and religion. It would not be easy to find among us a man who has won a purer fame; and I am happy to offer this tribute, because I would do something, no matter how little, to hasten the time when the spirit of Christian humanity shall be accounted an essential attribute and the brightest ornament of a public man.

"He returns to Washington, and is immediately ordered to the Cherokee nation, to take charge of the very difficult and hazardous task to his own fame of removing those savages from their native land. Some of his best friends regretted, most sincerely, that he had been ordered on this service; and, knowing the disposition of the world to cavil and complain without cause, had great apprehensions that he would lose a portion of the popularity he had acquired by his distinguished success on the Canadian frontier. But, behold the manner in which this last work has been performed! There is so much of noble generosity of character about Scott, independent of his skill and bravery as a soldier, that his life has really been one of romantic beauty and interest."

CHAPTER XXIV.

IT was about this time that the autobiographer was, without wish or agency on his part, brought into the arena of party politics, although long before a quiet Whig. A convention of delegates of that party met early in December, 1839, at Harrisburg, to select candidates for the Presidency and Vice-Presidency at the election in November of the following year.

Mr. Clay, the head of the party, and General Harrison were the principals before the convention. Scott had also a respectable number of supporters (the delegates of five States, including those of New York) in that body; but Scott wrote a number of letters to members, friends of Mr. Clay, to be seen by all, expressing the hope that the latter might, with any prospect of success, before the people, be selected as the candidate, and if not, that General Harrison might be the nominee.

So far as respects the younger, or third candidate, himself, the result is not, at this day, worth a single remark. But the accidental circumstances which finally ruled the convention, are too curious within themselves, as well as too important to the future of the country, to be longer suppressed.

There was abundant evidence from the beginning of the convention that Scott was the second choice of a great majority both of the Clay and Harrison members; but Mr. Leigh (the Honorable B. W.), who led the Virginia delegation, and that led the other Clay delegations—all Southern and Southwestern men;—by a singular infelicity, contrived that those delegations should lose both their first and second preferences. The supporters of Scott, after a great many ballotings, communicated to the separate assemblages of the Clay men, that if the latter did not, after the next vote, come over to Scott, their known second choice, they, the

New Yorkers and associates, would, in that case, next vote for Harrison, their second choice. Here the strangeness alluded to must be told.

Mr. Leigh—a man of perfect uprightness of character, of high abilities; and early in life a passionate and successful cultivator of polite literature—had now, and for many years before, become the slave of his profession—without any diminution of business, but with a yearly decrease of fees and increase of family — so fagged, for twelve and fourteen hours a day, that his acquaintance with the advancing world, literature, and politics, did not extend beyond the narrow circle of Richmond. Being without a rival in that sphere, and now for the first time in his life three days north of Washington;—conscious of the purity of his intentions, and having made up his own mind that Mr. Clay ought to be the next President, he carefully avoided everybody likely to perplex and distress him with the contrary wishes or calculations.

Congress met three days before the convention. The Whig members of the former, desirous of conversing understandingly with their friends as they passed through Washington to Harrisburg, held informal meetings, by States, and came to the conclusion, after inquiry and reflection, that Mr. Clay could scarcely carry a district represented by one of them—Mitchell, alone, being confident that his, the Lockport or Niagara District of New York, would vote for the illustrious Kentuckian; but Mitchell could not be relied upon; for he was long before the election put into the State prison as a forger.

Mr. Leigh, apprehending such interference at Washington, and true to his provincial superiority, quietly passed down the James River and up the Chesapeake Bay, through Baltimore, with a large number of dependent delegates, to Harrisburg — where he was taken possession of by two veteran and inveterate Clay supporters from the city of New York (traders in politics, but not members of the convention), who so mesmerized him that he could not believe a word said to him by men of the highest standing in the North and East. Hence, when the message, just mentioned, was received by the Clay supporters, that is, by Mr. Leigh, who was not only the organ, but the sole voice of that party, his mesmerizers told him to treat it with contempt, that it was a mere fetch, and that the Scott delegates would be obliged in a few ballots more to vote for Mr. Clay.

This assurance was speedily falsified, and then some

of the dupes, including Mr. Leigh himself—wished to move for a reconsideration of the vote; but Scott's friends very judiciously said, "No; it is too late. Harrison's name, as our nominee, will, in five minutes, be on the wings of the winds to all parts of the Union, and now to nominate another would distract the party and make us contemptible."

But the nomination and success of General Harrison, if his life had been spared some four years longer, would have been no detriment to his country. With excellent intentions and objects, and the good sense to appoint able counsellors, the country would not have been retarded in its prosperity, nor disgraced by corruption in high places. No one can, of course, be held responsible for sudden deaths among men. A single month in office, ended President Harrison's life, when the affecting plaint of Burke occurred to all: "What shadows we are, what shadows we pursue!"

Mr. Leigh's great error at Harrisburg is yet to be narrated, and referred to the same virtues combined with the inaptitude of one long ignorant of the world. All the able men who voted early or late for Harrison, were inclined to name Mr. Leigh, as a slight indemnification to Mr. Clay, for the Vice-Presidency;—but Mr.

Tyler, of the same delegation, wept audibly for the loss of Virginia's candidate, and intrigued quietly with the weaker brethren to secure that honor for himself. Mr. Leigh being sole committee man of his delegation on the selection of candidates, and the reverenced adviser of many others, delicately hesitated about receiving the nomination, and worse, from delicacy toward a colleague, neglected to tell distant members how utterly unfit Mr. Tyler was for the second place in the Government—nobody, of course, thinking of a vacancy in the presidential chair,—a case that had never occurred. Thus by the double squeamishness of a good man, the United States lost an eventual President not inferior to more than one man that had ever filled that high place.

Of Mr. Tyler's administration of the executive branch of the Government, but little will be said here. He soon committed the grossest tergiversation in politics, from the fear of Mr. Clay as a competitor for the succession, and to win that for himself, all the patronage of the Government, all the chips, shavings, and sweepings of office, down to the lowest clerkship, the posts of messengers and watchmen, were brought into market and bartered for support at the next election.

To the honor of the country, Mr. Tyler was allowed to relapse into a private station.

In June, 1841, Scott was, on the death of Major-General Macomb, called to reside in Washington as the General-in-Chief of the entire army. In that capacity he made several ordinary tours of inspection, but nothing occurred in the next five years that called him to any mission of importance. Many specimens of orders might be given to show his regard for the soldier, as well as love of military discipline and efficiency; but they would not be interesting to the general reader. One only will here be inserted to exhibit his long persevering and successful efforts to stop arbitrary, that is, illegal, punishments in the army.

GENERAL ORDERS.　　　　　　HEADQUARTERS OF THE ARMY,
No. 53.　　　　　　　　　WASHINGTON, *August* 20, 1842.

1. . . . . Intimations, through many channels, received at General Headquarters, lead to more than a suspicion that blows, kicks, cuffs, and lashes, against law, the good of the service and the faith of Government, have, in many instances, down to a late period,

16

been inflicted upon private soldiers of the army by their officers and non-commissioned officers.

2. . . . Inquiries into the reported abuses are in progress, with instructions, if probable evidence of guilt be found, to bring the offenders to trial.

3. . . . It is well known to every vigilant officer that discipline *can* be maintained (—and it *shall* be so maintained—) *by legal means.* Other resorts are, in the end, always destructive of good order and subordination.

4. . . . Insolence, disobedience, mutiny, are the usual provocations to unlawful violence. But these several offences are denounced by the 6th, 7th, and 9th of the rules and articles of war, and made punishable by the sentence of courts-martial. Instead, however, of waiting for such judgment, according to the nature and degree of guilt, deliberately found—the hasty and conceited—losing all self-control and dignity of command—assume that their individual importance is more outraged than the majesty of law, and act, at once, as legislators, judges, and executioners. Such gross usurpation is not to be tolerated in any well-governed army.

5. . . . For insolent words, addressed to a superior,

let the soldier be ordered into confinement. This, of itself, if followed by prompt repentance and apology, may often be found a sufficient punishment. If not, a court can readily authorize the final remedy. A deliberate, or unequivocal breach of orders, is treated with yet greater judicial rigor; and, in a clear case of mutiny, the sentence would, in all probability, extend to life. It is evident, then, that there is not even a pretext for punishments decreed on individual assumption, and at the dictate of pride and resentment.

6. . . . . But it may be said, in the case of mutiny, or conduct tending to this great crime—that it is necessary to cut down, on the spot, the exciter or ringleader. *First* order him to be seized. If his companions put him into irons or confinement, it is plain there is no spread of the dangerous example. But, should *they* hesitate;—or should it be necessary in any case of disobedience, desertion, or running away—*the object being to secure the person for trial;*—as always to repel a personal assault, or to stop an affray—in every one of these cases any superior may strike and wound; but only to the extent clearly necessary to such lawful end. Any excess, wantonly committed beyond such measured violence, would, itself, be punishable in the supe-

rior. No other case can possibly justify any superior in committing violence upon the body of any inferior, without the judgment of a court—except that it may sometimes be necessary, by force, to iron prisoners for security, or to gag them for quiet.

7. . . . Harsh and abusive words, passionately or wantonly applied to unoffending inferiors, is but little less reprehensible. Such language is, at once, unjust, vulgar, and unmanly; and, in this connection, it may be useful to recall a passage from the old *General Regulations for the Army* (by Scott):

" The general deportment of officers toward juniors or inferiors will be carefully watched and regulated. If this be cold or harsh, on the one hand, or grossly familiar on the other, the harmony or discipline of the corps cannot be maintained. The examples are numerous and brilliant, in which the most conciliatory manners have been found perfectly compatible with the exercise of the strictest command; and the officer who does not unite a high degree of moral vigor with the civility that springs from the heart, cannot too soon choose another profession in which imbecility would be less conspicuous, and harshness less wounding and oppressive." (*Edition* 1825.)

8. . . . . Government not only reposes " special trust and confidence in the patriotism, valor, fidelity, and abilities of" army officers, as is expressed on the face of commissions; but also in their self-control, respect for law and gentlemanly conduct on all occasions. A failure under either of those heads ought always to be followed by the loss of a commission.

9. . . . . At a time when, notwithstanding the smallness of the establishment, thousands of the most promising youths are desirous of military commissions, the country has a right to demand—not merely the usual exact observance of laws, regulations, and orders, but yet more—that every officer shall give himself up entirely to the cultivation and practice of all the virtues and accomplishments which can elevate an honorable profession. There is in the army of the United States, neither room, nor associates, for the idle, the ignorant, the vicious, the disobedient. To the very few such, thinly scattered over the service—whether in the line or the staff—these admonitions are mainly addressed; and let the vigilant eye of all commanders be fixed upon them. No bad or indifferent officer should receive from a senior any favor or indulgence whatsoever.

10. . . . . The attention of commanders of departments, regiments, companies, and garrisons is directed to the 101st of the rules and articles of war, which requires that the whole series shall be read to the troops at least once in every six months.

WINFIELD SCOTT.

In this interval of comparative inactivity, high army rank again came to be considered useless and burdensome. Several movements were made in the House of Representatives, to cut down Scott's long-fixed pay and emoluments, and one, quite formidable, in its inception, to abolish his office.

A previous motion to reduce his pay, etc., was defeated by a side battery, opened by the Hon. Charles J. Ingersoll, member of the House from Philadelphia. There was another bill lying on the clerk's table touching the daily compensation of the members of both Houses of Congress, and Mr. Ingersoll argued that the latter should first become a law, before Congress could, with decency, cut down the pay of the army.

Both propositions affecting Scott came to a definite vote in the House of Representatives, March, 1844.

Mr. Adams (J. Q.) "felt bound to declare that he did think it a very ill reward for the great and eminent services of that officer [Scott] during a period of thirty-odd years, in which there were some as gallant exploits as our history could show, and in which he had not spared to shed his blood, as well as for more recent services of great importance in time of peace—services of great difficulty and great delicacy—now to turn him adrift at his advanced age."

In respect to the reduction of his pay, etc., Mr. Adams " could not a moment harbor in his heart the thought that General Scott, if he had received from Government thousands of dollars more than he had, would have received one dollar which he did not richly deserve at the hands of his country."—*National Intelligencer*, *March* 30, 1844.

" Mr. C. J. Ingersoll wished to add but a single word. Perhaps he was the only member present who could recollect the day when this same General Scott had been the first man to show that the disciplined soldiery of our own country were fully able to cope with the trained troops of a foreign nation. When gentlemen were about to legislate General Scott out of office, he must be permitted to add one consideration to those which had so properly been stated by the venerable gentleman from Massachusetts (Mr. Adams), and it was this: That, while we were sitting here very coolly giving votes to legislate General Scott out of office, we ought not quite to forget that it was by virtue of his brave achievements we possessed the opportunity of voting here at all. It was easy for gentlemen to call those ' caterpillars ' who, in the hour of peril, had been the ' pillars ' of the public trust. He should be sorry indeed that this blow should fall upon the man who had struck the first blow in that struggle through which alone this Government had been preserved in being down to this hour. But it was obvious that neither office nor officer was in the slightest danger."—*National Intelligencer, March* 30, 1844.

Both propositions were voted down by large majorities.

It may be remarked that Mr. Adams and Mr. Ingersoll, in a common service of six years on the same floor of Congress, scarcely ever before agreed on any subject whatever. Indeed Mr. C. J. Ingersoll was an object of unusual hatred with the Whig party generally. Dr. Johnson "loved a good hater," and Mr. Ingersoll, to do him justice, fully repaid the Whigs in kind. Yet he was always to the autobiographer a valuable friend. Their acquaintance and friendship commenced early in the War of 1812, when no man, in the House of Representatives, struck more valiantly for his country than Mr. Ingersoll.

During a residence of some three years in Philadelphia, beginning in 1819, and always afterward, when on a visit to that city, Scott, perhaps never failed, a single Sunday, to be invited to Mr. Ingersoll's hospitable table, after the second church, where were met the usual guests — Judge Hopkinson, the author of *Hail Columbia;* Nicholas Biddle (two of the most accomplished and amiable men in America), Joseph Bonaparte, James Brown, Ex-Senator and Minister to France, and any stranger of eminence that might be passing through. In all these agreeable reunions, Mr. Ingersoll, a good scholar and linguist, bore his part well—giving and receiving pleasure.

CHAPTER XXV.

LETTER ON SLAVERY—TRACTS ON PEACE AND WAR—MR.
POLK PRESIDENT.

SCOTT's views on the question of negro slavery are
strongly alluded to, but not fully developed, in the
foregoing narrative. Begging the reader to forgive a
partial repetition of the same ideas and expressions, he
inserts his formal letter on the subject here:

WASHINGTON, *February* 9, 1843.

DEAR SIR:

I have been waiting for an evening's leisure to
answer your letter before me, and, after an unreason-
able delay, am at last obliged to reply in the midst of
official occupations.

That I ever have been named in connection with the Presidency of the United States, has not, I can assure *you*, the son of an ancient neighbor and friend, been by any contrivance or desire of mine; and certainly I shall never be in the field for that high office unless placed there *by a regular nomination.* Not, then, being a candidate, and seeing no near prospect of being *made* one, I ought, perhaps, to decline troubling you or others with my humble opinions on great principles of State Rights and Federal Administration; but as I cannot plead ignorance of the partiality of a few friends, in several parts of the Union, who may, by possibility, in a certain event, succeed in bringing me within the field from which a Whig candidate is to be selected, I prefer to err on the side of frankness and candor, rather than, by silence, to allow any stranger unwittingly to commit himself to my support.

Your inquiries open the whole question of domestic slavery, which has, in different forms, for a number of years, agitated Congress and the country.

Premising that you are the first person who has interrogated me on the subject, I give you the basis of what *would* be my reply in greater detail, if time allowed and the contingency alluded to above were less remote.

In boyhood, at William and Mary College, and in common with most, if not all, my companions, I became deeply impressed with the views given by Mr. Jefferson, in his "Notes on Virginia," and by Judge Tucker, in the Appendix to his edition of Blackstone's Commentaries, in favor of a gradual emancipation of slaves. That Appendix I have not seen in thirty odd years, and, in the same period, have read scarcely anything on the subject; but my early impressions are fresh and unchanged. Hence, if I had had the honor of a seat in the Virginia Legislature in the winter of 1831–'2, when a bill was brought forward to carry out those views, I should certainly have given it my hearty support.

I suppose I scarcely need say that, in my opinion, Congress has no color of authority, under the Constitution, for touching the relation of master and slave within a State.

I hold the opposite opinion in respect to the District of Columbia. Here, with the consent of the owners, or on the payment of "just compensation," Congress may legislate at its discretion. But my conviction is equally strong that, unless it be step by step with the Legislatures of Virginia and Maryland, it would be dangerous to both races in those States to touch the relation between master and slave in this District.

. I have from the first been of opinion that Congress was bound by the Constitution to receive, to refer, and to report upon petitions relating to domestic slavery as in the case of all other petitions; but I have not failed to see and to regret the unavoidable irritation which the former have produced in the Southern States, with the consequent peril to the two colors, whereby the adoption of any plan of emancipation has everywhere among us been greatly retarded.

I own, myself, no slave; but never have attached blame to masters for not liberating their slaves—well knowing that liberation, without the means of sending them in comfort to some position favorable to " the pursuit of happiness," would, in most cases, be highly injurious to all around, as well as to the manumitted families themselves—unless the operation were general and under the auspices of prudent legislation. But I am persuaded that it is a high moral obligation of masters and slaveholding States to employ all means, not incompatible with the safety of both colors, to meliorate slavery even to extermination.

It is gratifying to know that general melioration has been great, and is still progressive, notwithstanding the disturbing causes alluded to above. The more direct process of emancipation may, no doubt, be earlier commenced and quickened in some communities than in others. Each, I do not question, has the right to judge for itself, both as to time and means, and I consider interference or aid from without, except on invitation from authority within, to be as hurtful to the sure progress of melioration, as it may be fatal to the lives of vast multitudes of all ages, sexes, and colors. The work of liberation cannot be *forced* without such horrid results. Christian philanthropy is ever mild and considerate. Hence all violence ought to be deprecated by the friends of religion and humanity. Their persuasions cannot fail at the right time to free the master from the slave, and the slave from the master; perhaps before the latter shall have found out and acknowledged that the relation between the parties had long been mutually prejudicial to their worldly interests.

There is no evil without, in the order of Providence, some compensating benefit. The bleeding African was torn from his savage home by his ferocious neighbors, sold into slavery, and cast upon this continent. Here, in the mild South, the race has wonderfully multiplied, compared with anything ever known in barbarous life. The descendants of a few thousands have become many millions; and all, from the first, made acquainted with the arts of civilization, and, above all, brought under the light of the Gospel.

From the promise made to Abraham, some two thousand years had elapsed before the advent of our Saviour, and the Israelites, the chosen people of God, were, for wise purposes, suffered to remain in bondage longer than Africans have been on our shore. This race has already experienced the resulting compensations alluded to; and, as the white missionary has never been able to penetrate the dark regions of Africa, or to establish himself in its interior, it may be within the scheme of Providence that the great work of spreading the Gospel over that vast continent, with all the arts and comforts of civilization, is to be finally accomplished by the black man restored from American bondage. A foothold there has already been gained for him, and in such a scheme centuries are but as seconds to Him who moves worlds as man moves a finger.

I do but *suggest* the remedies and consolations of slavery, to inspire patience, hope, and charity on all sides. The mighty subject calls for the exercise of all man's wisdom and virtue, and these may not suffice without aid from a higher source.

It is in the foregoing manner, my dear sir, that I have long been in the habit, in conversation, of expressing myself, all over our common country, on the question of negro slavery, and I must say that I have found but very few persons to differ with me, however opposite their geographical positions.

Such are the views or opinions which you seek. I cannot suppress or mutilate them, although now liable to be more generally known. Do with them what you please. I neither court nor shun publicity.

I remain, very truly, yours,

WINFIELD SCOTT.

T. P. Atkinson, Esq., Danville, Virginia.

Peace and War.

WASHINGTON, *March* 24, 1845.

I have received your letter of the 21st instant, accompanied by certain proceedings of the General Peace Convention.

My participation in war, as well as endeavors on several occasions to preserve peace, without sacrificing the honor and the interests of my country, are matters of public history. These antecedents, together with my sentiments on the abstract question of *peace and war*, inserted a year ago in a Peace Album, and since published, I learn, in several journals, might be offered as a sufficient reply to your communication.

I have always maintained the moral right to wage a just and necessary war, and, consequently, the wisdom and humanity, as applicable to the United States, in the present state of the world, of *defensive* preparations. If the principal nations of the earth liable to come in conflict with us in our natural growth and just pursuits, can be induced to disarm, I should be happy to see the United States follow the example. But without a general agreement to that effect, and a strong probability that it would be carried out in good faith by others, I am wholly opposed to giving up *home preparation*, and the natural and Christian right of *self-defence*.

The published sentiments alluded to may not have fallen under your observation. I enclose a copy.

I remain respectfully,

Your most obedient servant,

WINFIELD SCOTT.

J. C. BECKWITH, ESQ., Corresponding Secretary.

[Written in a Peace Album.]

Peace and War.

If war be the natural state of savage tribes, peace is the first want of every civilized community. War no doubt is, under any circumstances, a great calamity; yet submission to outrage would often be a greater calamity. Of the two parties to any war, one, at least, must be in the wrong—not unfrequently both. An error in such an issue is, on the part of chief magistrates, ministers of state, and legislators having a voice in the question, a crime of the greatest magnitude. The slaying of an individual by an individual is, in comparative guilt, but a drop of blood. Hence the highest moral obligation to treat national differences with temper, justice, and fairness; always to see that the cause of war is not only *just* but *sufficient;* to be sure that we do not *covet* our neighbor's lands, "nor any thing that is his;" that we are as ready to give as to demand explanation, apology, indemnity; in short, we should especially remember, "All things whatsoever ye would that men should do to you, do ye even so to them." This divine precept is of universal obligation: it is as applicable to rulers, in their transactions with other nations, as to private individuals in their daily intercourse with each other. Power is intrusted by " the Author of peace and lover of concord," to do good and to avoid evil. Such, clearly, is the revealed will of God.

WINFIELD SCOTT.

WASHINGTON, *April* 26, 1844.

On the approach of the next Presidential election, it was agreed by all Whigs, the chances of success seeming favorable, to leave the field without a convention to Mr. Clay; but Mr. Polk was chosen and inaugurated March 4, 1845.

Mr. Tyler, doubtless, like several of his successors, was weaker in office than Mr. Polk, whose little strength lay in the most odious elements of the human character—*cunning and hypocrisy.* It is true that these qualities, when discovered, become positive weaknesses; but they often triumph over wisdom and virtue before discovery. It may be added that a man of meaner presence is not often seen. He was, however, virtually, the nominee of General Jackson.

CHAPTER XXVI.

HOSTILITIES with Mexico, might, perhaps, have been avoided; but Texas lay between—or rather in the scale of war.

At an advanced stage of the diplomatic quarrel, Brigadier-General .Taylor was ordered, with a respectable number of regular troops, to Corpus Christi, near the Mexican frontier, as a good point of observation. This selection of the commander was made with the concurrence of the autobiographer, who, knowing him to be slow of thought, of hesitancy in speech, and unused to the pen, took care, about the same time, to provide him, unsolicited, with a staff officer, Captain

(subsequently, Lieutenant-Colonel) Bliss, his exact com-
plement, who superadded modest, quiet manners, which
qualities could not fail to win the confidence of his
peculiar commander, and on which usefulness entirely
depended. The whole intent was a success: the combination of the general and the chief of his staff working like a charm. Though, perhaps, somewhat in
advance of chronology, a little fuller sketch of one of
the most fortunate of men, may here not be out of
place. The autobiographer knew him well.

General Taylor's elevation to the Presidency, the
result of military successes, though a marvel, was not a
curse to his country. Mr. Webster, in his strong idio-
matic English, said of the nomination that it was "not
fit to be made;" but probably he would have been
equally dissatisfied with any candidate other than himself.

With a good store of common sense, General Taylor's mind had not been enlarged and refreshed by
reading, or much converse with the world. Rigidity
of ideas was the consequence. The frontiers and small
military posts had been his home. Hence he was quite
ignorant, for his rank, and quite bigoted in his ignorance. His simplicity was childlike, and with innumer-

able prejudices—amusing and incorrigible—well suited to the tender age. Thus if a man, however respectable, chanced to wear a coat of an unusual color, or his hat a little on one side of the head;—or an officer to leave the corner of his handkerchief dangling from an outside pocket—in any such case, this critic held the offender to be a coxcomb—perhaps, something worse, whom he would not, to use his oft-repeated phrase, "touch with a pair of tongs." Any allusion to literature much beyond good old Dilworth's Spelling Book, on the part of one wearing a sword, was evidence, with the same judge, of utter unfitness for heavy marchings and combats. In short, few men have ever had a more comfortable, labor-saving contempt for learning of every kind.* Yet this old soldier and neophyte statesman, had the true basis of a great character:—pure, uncorrupted morals, combined with indomitable courage. Kind-hearted, sincere, and hospitable in a plain way, he had no vice but prejudice, many friends, and left behind him not an enemy in the world—not even in

---

* Marlborough, one of the greatest generals of any age, and the first diplomat and courtier of his own, was also without science and literature—knowing nothing of history except the little he picked up at the acting of some of Shakspeare's dramas.

the autobiographer, whom, in the blindness of his great weakness, he—*after* being named for the Presidency— had seriously wronged.

Ought this, charitably, to be supposed an unconscious error, or placed to a different account?

" To keep the proud thy friend, see that thou do him not a service:
  For, behold, he will hate thee for his debt."
Prov. Philosophy.

As early as May, 1846, when it was known that the Mexicans had assumed a threatening attitude on the Rio Grande, an inclination to send Scott to that frontier was intimated. He replied, 1. That it was harsh and unusual for a senior, without reënforcements, to supersede a meritorious junior; 2. That he doubted whether that was the right season, or the Rio Grande the right basis for *offensive* operations against Mexico; and suggested the plan of conquering a peace which he ultimately executed.

Leading Democrats took alarm at the appointment of a Whig to so high a trust—fearing, as they did him the honor to say—his " knack at success," and caused Mr. Polk to doubt and reject his views. Whereupon Scott intimated that without the approval of his plan of campaign, and the steady confidence and support of the Government, he would not be able to conduct any expedition to advantage; for soldiers had a far greater dread of a fire upon the rear, than of the most formidable enemy in front. The President at once caused him to be relieved from the proposed mission.

At this period, Scott usually—as always in troublous times—spent from fifteen to eighteen hours a day in his office, happened, on being called upon by the Secretary of War to be found absent. In explanation, Scott hurriedly wrote a note to say that he was back in the office, having only stepped out, for the moment, to take—regular meals being out of the question —" a hasty plate of soup." This private note being maliciously thrown into party newspapers, all the witlings—forgetting their own *hasty* pudding, fastened upon it, with much glee, and also tried their clumsy wit on the phrase "conquer a peace;" but not *after* the early fact, as also on the " fire upon the rear;" but never *after* the fire of the enemy and that of the Administration, on front and rear, had been silenced by the campaign of 1847.

These were no *trivialities* in their day; for, by the aid of party madness and malice they came very near destroying Scott's usefulness in the Mexican war.

17

Taylor's early successes on this side of the Rio Grande, so handsomely reported by Bliss, won him great favor with the country. A resolution giving him the thanks of Congress, and a sword was promptly introduced. Scott hastened to address a circular (private) note to a dozen members of the two Houses of Congress —including the Kentucky Senators, and Mr. Jefferson Davis—arguing that the gold medal ought to be substituted for the sword—being the higher honor, and eminently Taylor's due. The suggestion was adopted, and further to show that Scott did not neglect the hero of the Rio Grande, he annexes the following report:

"HEADQUARTERS OF THE ARMY,
WASHINGTON, *July* 25, 1846.

" HON. W. L. MARCY, Secretary of War:

[*Endorsed by Major-General Scott, on the Resolution of Congress voting a medal to Major-General Taylor, which Resolution the Secretary had referred to General Scott.*]

" As medals are among the surest monuments of history, as well as muniments of individual distinction, there should be given to them, besides intrinsic value and durability of material the utmost grace of design, with the highest finish in mechanical execution. All this is necessary to give the greater or adventitious value; as in the present instance, the medal is to be, at once, an historical record and a reward of distinguished merit. The credit of the donor thus becomes even more than that of the receiver interested in obtaining a perfect specimen in the fine arts.

" The within resolution prescribes *gold* as the material of the medal. The general form (circular) may be considered as equally settled by our own practice, and that of most nations, ancient and modern. There is, however, some little diversity in *diameter* and *thickness* in the medals heretofore ordered by Congress, at different periods, as may be seen in the cabinets of the War and Navy Departments. Diversity in dimensions is even greater in other countries.

" The specific character of the medal is shown by its two faces, or the *face* and the *reverse*. The within resolution directs ' appropriate devices and inscriptions thereon.'

" For the *face*, a bust likeness is needed, to give, with the name and the rank of the donee, *individual-*

ity. To obtain the likeness, a first-rate miniature painter should, of course, be employed.

"The reverse receives the device, appropriate to the events commemorated. To obtain this, it is suggested that the resolutions and despatches, belonging to the subject, be transmitted to a master in the art of design—say Professor Weir, at West Point—for a drawing—including, if practicable, this inscription:

PALO ALTO;

RESACA DE LA PALMA:

May 8 and 9, 1846.

"A third artist—all to be well paid—is next to be employed—a die sinker. The mint of the United States will do the coinage.

"Copies, in cheaper metal, of all our gold medals, should be given to the libraries of the Federal and State Governments, to those of colleges, etc.

"The medals voted by the Revolutionary Congress were executed—designs and dies—under the superintendence of Mr. Jefferson, in Paris, about the year 1786. Those struck in honor of victories, in our war of 1812, were all—at least so far as it respected the land service—done at home, and not one of them presented, I think, earlier than the end of Mr. Monroe's Administration (1825). The delay principally resulted from the want of good die sinkers. There was only one of mediocre merit (and he a foreigner) found for the army. What the state of this art may now be in the United States I know not. But I beg leave again to suggest that the honor of the country requires that medals, voted by Congress, should always exhibit the arts, involved, in their highest state of perfection *wherever* found; for letters, science, and the fine arts constitute but *one* republic, embracing the world. So thought our early Government, and Mr. Jefferson — a distinguished member of that general republic.

" All which is respectfully submitted to the Secretary of War."

But before his written solicitude about the medal— in May—the day on which the news of Taylor's first victories (two) arrived—a number of leading Whigs (not including Mr. Clay or Mr. Webster) in a panic, .about the soup, called upon the autobiographer to inquire whether Taylor was a Whig or not, and whether he might not advantageously be Scott's substitute as their next Presidential candidate? More amused than offended at their cowardice and candor, Scott gave emphatically, all the points in the foregoing sketch of the then rising general, omitting (it is believed) any allusion to his lack of general information, and added, as a striking proof of his honesty this anecdote:

Early in the times of Jacksonism, in Kentucky, the demagogues broke the Constitution, and the supréme judges of the State, together; set up a new supreme court of their own, and a rag bank without a dollar in specie—literally to " emit bills of credit " in violation of the Constitution of the United States. Money (bills of credit) being superabundant, a wild spirit of speculation became general running into madness, soon followed by coextensive bankruptcy and ruin. Colonel Zachary Taylor chanced to visit Louisville (his home) in the height of the speculation; but though not infected himself, he was induced to endorse a heavy obligation of a friend, which, of course, in due time fell upon him. He resolutely refused to take any relief from the stop-laws of the same demagogues, or to pay in their rag currency, and although a dear lover of money, persistently paid his endorsement in specie. In continuation, Scott stated that being in Louisville, in the command of the Western Department of the army, he gave the colonel the short leave of absence that brought him there with the heavy bags which finally freed him from debt. The parting with the cash agonized him not a little, but soon he recovered, and the next moment felt happy in his double-proof integrity.

And had Scott no trial of his own? The statement, just given fixed Taylor as the next Whig candidate for the Presidency; but Scott, without murmur or petulance, did not fail to make his backsliding Whig friends feel their inferiority. Never had he been better self-poised, and to his last hour he cannot fail to point to this period of obloquy on the part of enemies and desertion of friends, as by far the most heroic of his life. Happily by the ruling of Providence, that, and other defeats in politics, have proved to him blessings in disguise. Whether, looking to subsequent events, the country has equally profited by the results, he has the vanity to doubt.

By extraordinary importunities from Washington, one object being to decry Scott's plea for adequate preparation, and his doubts as to the line of operations from the Rio Grande—aided by a letter from that man of rare abilities and every moral excellence— John J. Crittenden—written at Scott's desk; and which he read with a dissenting smile—Taylor was told to say no more of reënforcements and means of transportation ; but, added Crittenden—" the public is impatient ; take foot in hand and off for the Halls of Montezuma."   Thus stimulated, Taylor, against his own judgment, marched under the greatest difficulties upon the little village of Monterey, which he captured (*cui bono ?*) and became *planted*—as it was impracticable —no matter with what force, to reach any vital part of Mexico by that route.   Accordingly, Taylor remained fast at Monterey and its neighborhood, with varying numbers, down to the peace.

Reliable information reached Washington, almost daily (see Taylor's own Reports, Ex. Doc. No. 60, H. of R., 30th Con., 1st Session), that the wild volunteers as soon as beyond the Rio Grande, committed, with impunity, all sorts of atrocities on the persons and property of Mexicans, and that one of the former, from a concealed position, had even shot a Mexican as he marched out of Monterey, under the capitulation.*

* This case was one reported by Taylor, who asked for advice. And

There was no legal punishment for any of those offences, for by the strange omission of Congress, American troops take with them beyond the limits of their own country, no law but the Constitution of the United States, and the rules and articles of war. These do not provide any court for the trial or punishment of murder, rape, theft, &c., &c.—no matter by whom, or on whom committed.

To suppress these disgraceful acts abroad, the autobiographer drew up an elaborate paper, in the form of an order—called, his *martial law order*—to be issued and enforced in Mexico, until Congress could be stimulated to legislate on the subject. On handing this paper to the Secretary of War (Mr. Marcy) for his approval, a *startle* at the title was the only comment he then, or ever made on the subject. It was soon silently returned, as too explosive for safe handling. A little later the Attorney-General called (at whose instance can only be guessed) and asked for a copy, and the law officer of the Government whose business it is to speak

what advice does the reader suppose the Secretary to have given? To execute the brute under martial law? No! Taylor was advised to send the monster home—that is, to reward him with a discharge! See the same document. (P. 369.) I had left Washington two days earlier.

17*

on all such matters, was stricken with legal dumbness. All the authorities were evidently alarmed at the proposition to establish martial law, even in a foreign country, occupied by American troops. Hence they touched the subject as daintily as a " terrier mumbles a hedgehog." I therefore was left in my own darkness on the subject. I sent the paper, however, to General Taylor, telling him frankly, that it had been seen by at least two members of the cabinet, but that it was not approved or disapproved by either, and for that reason it was not enjoined upon him, but left to his own responsibility to adopt it as his order or not, as he might think proper.

It is understood that Taylor on casting his eye slightly over the paper, and perceiving it contained what he termed, " a learned commentary on the military code," threw it aside—saying, " It is another of *Scott's Lessons*" or " *Novels*"—as his tactics and military institutes had been previously called by officers of a certain age (not West Point graduates) who deemed it a great hardship, late in life, to be obliged, for the first time, to study the simplest elements of their profession.

This paper will be inserted entire, in a subsequent part of this narrative: 1. On account of its history just given; 2. Because, without it, I could not have maintained the discipline and honor of the army, or have reached the capital of Mexico.

The martial law order was not published until the autobiographer was fairly out of the United States—at Tampico. It was successively republished at Vera Cruz, Puebla, and the capital, so that it might be familiarly known to every man in the army, and in a translation, it was also extensively circulated among the people of the country. Under it, all offenders, Americans and Mexicans, were alike punished—with death for murder or rape, and for other crimes proportionally. It will be seen that the order did not in the least interfere with the administration of justice between Mexican and Mexican, by the ordinary courts of the country. It only provided a special American tribunal for any case to which an American might be a party. And further, it should be observed, that military commissions in applying penalties to convicted felons, were limited to " *known* punishments, in like cases, in some of the States of the United States "—the latter, as such, being without a common law, or a common criminal code.

Notwithstanding the cowardice of certain high func-

tionaries on the subject, there has been no pursuit of
the author. On the contrary, it has been admitted by
all that the order worked like a charm; that it con-
ciliated Mexicans; intimidated the vicious of the
several races, and being executed with impartial rigor,
gave the highest moral deportment and discipline ever
known in an invading army.

CHAPTER XXVII.

SEVERAL times in the summer and autumn of 1846,
I repeated to the War Department my desire to be
ordered to Mexico at the head of a competent force.
At length my request was acceded to.

WAR DEPARTMENT, WASHINGTON,
November 23, 1846.

SIR :

The President, several days since, communicated
in person to you his orders to repair to Mexico, to take
the command of the forces there assembled, and particularly to organize and set on foot an expedition to
operate on the Gulf coast, if, on arriving at the theatre
of action, you shall deem it to be practicable. It is not

proposed to control your operations by definite and positive instructions, but you are left to prosecute them as your judgment, under a full view of all the circumstances, shall dictate. The work is before you, and the means provided, or to be provided, for accomplishing it, are committed to you, in the full confidence that you will use them to the best advantage.

The objects which it is desirable to obtain have been indicated, and it is hoped that you will have the requisite force to accomplish them.

Of this you must be the judge, when preparations are made, and the time for action arrived.

Very respectfully,

Your obedient servant,

W. L. MARCY,

Secretary of War.

General Winfield Scott.

From an early day—it is believed, the very beginning—the Secretary of the Treasury, Mr. Walker, and Mr. Secretary Marcy, were in favor of giving me the substantial direction of the war on land—each having often done me the honor to express his fullest confidence in my zeal and capacity for the occasion.

For a week prior to Mr. Marcy's letter, President Polk sent for me once or twice daily. In these interviews every expression of kindness and confidence was lavished upon me. Such was the warmth and emphasis of his professions, that he fully won my confidence. I gave him a cordial reciprocation of my personal sympathy and regard—being again and again assured that the country would be bankrupted and dishonored unless the war could be made plainly to march toward a successful conclusion, and that I only could give to it the necessary impetus and direction. Not to have been deceived by such protestations, would have been, in my judgment, unmanly suspicion and a crime. Accordingly, though oppressed with the labors of military preparation, I made time to write a circular to the leading Whigs in Congress (a few days before their meeting) to say how handsomely I had been treated by the President and Secretary of War—begging that the new regiments might be authorized.with the least possible delay, &c., &c.

In the very·act of embarking, at New Orleans, on the expedition, a stranger, Mr. Hodge of that city (since Assistant Secretary of the Treasury and a resident of Washington), saw me half a minute, to communicate a letter from my dear friend—Alexander Barrow—then a senator from Louisiana—saying that the President had asked for the grade of lieutenant-general, in order to place Senator Benton over me in the Army of Mexico. I begged that Mr. Barrow might be thanked for his kindness, but added that he must be mistaken about Mr. Benton; for if the rank were asked for, it could only—remembering Mr. Polk's assurances of support and reward—be intended for me on the report of my first success, and I continued, a short time longer, to carry on, besides the *official*, a *semi*-official correspondence, with the War Department, for the President, as before.

A grosser abuse of human confidence is nowhere recorded.

Mr. Polk's mode of viewing the case seems to have been this: " Scott is a Whig; therefore the Democracy is not bound to observe good faith with him. Scott is a Whig; therefore, his successes may be turned to the prejudice of the Democratic party. We must, however, profit by his military experience, and, if successful, by the force of patronage and other helps, contrive to crown Benton with the victory, and thus triumph both in the field and at the polls." This bungling treachery was planned during the precise period of my very friendly interviews with Mr. Polk! It soon became fully developed, and, in all essentials, acknowledged before Congress. The lieutenant-generalcy was, however, rejected, when Mr. Polk taxed his supporters to the utmost to procure for him authority to place a junior Major-General (Benton) over a senior (Scott), and was again ignominiously defeated—aided by the manly spirit of the same small number of Democrats.

This vile intrigue so disgusted Congress, and its defeat so depressed the zeal and influence of the Administration, that instead of authorizing the additional forces needed for the war at once, the augmentation was delayed till near the end of the session. This was the first fruit of bad faith or political blindness; for, in war, *time* is always a great element of success—sometimes the first.

I reached the Brazos San Iago, near the mouth of the Rio Grande, in Christmas week, and proceeded up that river to Camargo, which place or vicinage I had appointed for a meeting with Major-General Taylor by a communication that preceded me four days; but, by the gross neglect of the officer who bore it, it lost three of those days at that place. In the mean time Taylor made a strange digression, with a part of his troops, toward Tampico—for it was fully as difficult for an army to penetrate Mexico from that point, as from Monterey. But in either case, why divide his forces?

A fatality attended my communication to Taylor. It was most confidential, and so marked, outside and in—containing a sketch of my views and intentions. Yet at the volunteer headquarters, Monterey, it was opened, freely read and discussed by numbers—all not in a condition to be wise or discreet. The package being remade, it was next forwarded after Taylor by a very young officer with a few men, who was inveigled into Villa Gran and slain; his despatches taken, and received by Santa Anna before Taylor saw the duplicate.

The appointed meeting with Taylor, for harmonizing operations with him, after full discussion—having failed, by reason of his digression toward Tampico, and the blunders resulting in the loss of the despatches— was a great disappointment to me. In them, I had said, that he should have his choice of the two armies, that is, either remain as the immediate commander in Northern Mexico, or accompany me in the command of a division, to the capital, with every assurance, in either case, of confidence and support.

I had now, without the benefit of the consultation I had sought, to detach from the army of the Rio Grande such regular troops as I deemed indispensable to lead the heavier masses of volunteers and other green regiments, promised for the descent on Vera Cruz and the conquest of the capital—leaving Taylor a sufficient defensive force to maintain the false position at Monterey, and discretion to contract his line to the Rio Grande, with the same means of defence. This contraction, with a view to economize men and money, I certainly should have ordered at once, if Taylor had been present to support me; but as many of the wiseacres at Washington still preferred the short impracticable cut to "the Halls of Montezuma," *via* Monterey and San Luis Potosi—a blunder, concurred in at one time by Taylor;—and as I had then discovered that my friend Barrow's message by Mr. Hodge was well founded—that is, instead of a friend in the President, I had, in him, an enemy more to be dreaded than Santa Anna and all his hosts—I left the basis of operations or the line of defence in that quarter, in *statu quo*, but only with troops sufficient for the latter purpose.

Both Taylor and the Secretary of War had vacillated on all those points. Each for a time had inclined to a direct advance from the Rio Grande. Each had glanced at the Vera Cruz basis, an idea always mine; each had favored the defensive line of Monterey or the Sierra Madre; and Taylor, a little later, seemed to favor standing on the defensive on the banks of the Rio Grande, which he had left against his judgment. (See Executive Doc. No. 56.)

The Mexicans had never any apprehension of an effective invasion from that quarter or from Tampico. In respect to either of these routes, they might have expressed what the Russians felt when Napoleon marched upon Moscow: "Come unto us with few, and we will overwhelm you; come unto us with many, and you shall overwhelm yourselves." As to holding the line of the Sierra Madre or other line of defence, and standing fast, that would have been the worst possible state of things—"a little war," or "a war like a peace"—a perpetual condition; for Santa Anna would have regarded it as a mere scratch on the surface.

To compel a people, singularly obstinate, to *sue for peace*, it is absolutely necessary, as the sequel in this case showed, to strike, effectively, at the vitals of the nation.

The order for the troops to descend from Monterey

to the sea-coast, was issued at Camargo, Jan. 3, 1847, and I immediately returned to the Brazos San Jago.

It was this order, that, at first, caused the gentle regrets of Taylor, but soon began to sour his mind in proportion as he became more and more prominent as a candidate for the Presidency. Thus, after the peace, when coming North, and running the gantlet of universal cheers and praise, the ovation unhinged his mind, when, in replying to a flattering address, at a Pascagoula barbecue, he made this extraordinary speech :

" You have alluded to my being stripped of *my* troops on the Rio Grande; and my being left, as it might seem, at the mercy of the enemy, just before the battle of Buena Vista, renders it proper, probably, that I should make a few remarks in relation to that matter. I received at Victoria, while on my march to Tampico —a movement which I had advised the War Department I should make for certain reasons—an order from the General-in-Chief of the Army (Scott) stripping me of the greater part of my command, and particularly of regular troops and volunteers well instructed. The order was received by me with much surprise, and, I must confess, produced the strongest feelings of regret, mortification and disappointment, *as I knew that Santa Anna was in striking distance of my lines, with an army of 25,000—probably the best appointed men ever collected in Mexico.*"

The harmless errors, both of fact and opinion, of a good man, ought to be treated as a nurse treats a child —a little sick and a little spoiled—gently; but if his errors, springing from vanity and self-love, wound another, the injury is the deeper in proportion to the standing of the author, and, therefore, are to be dealt with unsparingly.

1. Elated with flattery, our hero

————" grew vain;
Fought all his battles o'er again;
And thrice he routed all his foes, and thrice he slew the slain."

He calls the army of the Rio Grande " my troops ! "

2. *He knew that Santa Anna, with an overwhelming force, was in striking distance.*

If so, he not only withheld the fact from the War Department and the General-in-Chief, but—I write it in sorrow—he actually, up to the last moment, gave the contrary assurance to both!

The proof:—some alarm, in front, having taken

him from Monterey to Saltillo, he writes thence, February 4: "I found everything quiet in our front."

*   *   *   *   *   *   *   *   *

"Indeed it is reported that a large portion of the troops, at San Luis, have taken the direction of Vera Cruz." . Ex. Document, 56. (Santa Anna had, some time before, received the captured despatches.) Three days later, Taylor wrote again (to me) at. the Brazos San Jago, to the like effect, and the same day, February 7, Document 56, p. 300, to the War Department: "There is understood to be no considerable force in our front, nor is it likely that any serious demonstration will be made in this direction. The frequent alarms" (in Worth's and Wood's camps)— always frequent in Worth's—"since the middle of December, seem to have been without foundation." Both of these letters were written at Agua Nueva, some eighteen miles in advance of Saltillo—his forces being a good deal scattered, notwithstanding my admonition, in concurrence with the War Department, to hold himself, while standing on the defensive, in a concentrated coil. One letter more of the same tenor, written (February 14), nine days before the battle of

Buena Vista, which reached the Brazos, when I was many days at sea, bent on conquest. In this letter—same Document, 56, p. 308—Taylor, at Agua Nueva, says: "Everything is quiet in and about Saltillo."

*   *   *   *   *   *   *   *   *

"Up to the 26th of January, the Mexican Congress had done nothing to supply the wants of the army, which had received nothing for January, and had but half the necessary funds for December. Rumors reach our camp, from time to time, of the projected advance of a Mexican force upon this position; but I think such a movement improbable!"

Those are sad self-contradictions! But are the uncharitable beyond the pale of Christian charity? Certainly not. Bliss wrote the despatches, about which the general knew but little, and remembered less; and not Bliss, but vanity, dictated the barbecue speech in question.

3. *He had been stripped, etc.—left at the mercy of the enemy!*

Indeed! but the facts: I left, under him, a small fraction less than seven thousand men, with a reasonable portion of regulars, including batteries of field

artillery—and other regiments soon expected, with,
advice to stand concentrated behind the stone walls
of Monterey, or to consider himself at liberty to take
up the impregnable line of the Rio Grande. The
defence of Texas was now the main purpose of this
army—it having been shown that even with his whole
force he could make no effective impression on Mexico
from that quarter. With this preface, my very sufficient defence shall again be quoted from reports under
General Taylor's own signature.

After the detached troops had reached the seaboard
he writes, from Monterey, January 27, 1847 (Ex. Doc.
No. 56, p. 292), "the force with which I am left, in
this quarter, though greatly deficient in regular troops,
will, doubtless, enable me to hold the positions now
occupied." Nothing more had been enjoined, nor was
expected, without large reënforcements, and *penetration*
had not been previously attempted, nor was attempted,
the following summer, when his numbers again became
formidable, although he solicited the War Department
for reënforcements (in his letter of February 14, before
quoted), and says he is "urging forward supplies; for,
if joined by a sufficient force of new regiments, I wish
to be able to take any opportunity that may offer to

make a diversion in favor of Major-General Scott's operations." (All have heard of a pavement of good intentions!) After awhile he got the regiments (and kept them from me), making his numbers eight thousand effectives—I being in Puebla at the time, with rather less than fifty-five hundred—in the heart of the enemy's country—cut loose (by the want of numbers) from the coast, and only with one other small detachment, left at Jalapa. General Taylor now quite at his ease, writes coolly and leisurely to the War Department from Monterey, June 16: "In my communication of May 28 (Ex. Doc. 56, p. 387), I had reason to present my views in relation to operations against San Luis Potosi, at least in regard to the minimum force (six thousand or eight thousand) with which I thought they could be undertaken. I shall prepare the force under my orders for service in that direction, should it be found expedient and practicable thus to operate; but [!] I may be permitted to question the utility of moving, at a very heavy expense over an extremely long line and having no communication with the main column operating from Vera Cruz [!]. If I were called upon to make a suggestion on the general subject of operations against Mexico, it would certainly be to hold, in this quarter [Monterey] a *defensive* line, and throw all the remaining troops into the other column!!" Then why the clamor about being "stripped?" why his clamor for reënforcements by which Brigadier-General Cadwallader and three regiments were diverted from me? why not attempt a feint toward San Luis Potosi, even if the advance had been forced to stop at a fourth or a fifth of the distance; and, above all—why detain so long the reënforcements of Cadwallader's and other brigades I so much needed!! A farther delay was incurred waiting for the Secretary's concurrence, dated July 15, and, finally, most of those reënforcements came to me long after the war was finished, and the dictated or conquered peace, was actually in preparation for signature. And thus my rivals and enemies were, at a late day, forced to acknowledge, practically, the justness of my early plans, views, and predictions!

4. One more remark on a point in the same barbacue speech: *Santa Anna's twenty-five thousand well appointed army at Buena Vista.*

It is true that Santa Anna in summoning Taylor to surrender, gives, to intimidate (a hopeless endeavor), his strength at twenty-five thousand; but four days before the battle of Buena Vista the Mexican official return of his forces, dated at Encarnacion, puts down his total numbers at fourteen thousand and forty-eight, all told, including sick and lame (more than two thousand) and the remainder, half famished with thirst and hunger. General Taylor, too, giving his reasons for not concentrating his army at Monterey, as he was advised to do—preferring the advanced position of Agua Nueva, says it was in order "to fight the Mexican general, immediately after he had crossed the desert country [about one hundred and fifty miles in extent] which lay just in my front, and before he could have time to refresh and recruit his army." This seems not to be bad reasoning; but suppose the Americans had been concentrated within the strong walls of Monterey; —the repulse of the enemy would have been more certain and more crippling, with less loss on our part, beside saving the battle of Buena Vista, and by delaying Santa Anna, the battle of Cerro Gordo, and hastening the capture of "the Halls of Montezuma." The victory of Buena Vista, was, no doubt, glorious in itself, and resounded as such all over America and Europe; but, as has been said of the barren capitulation of Monterey—*cui bono?* It did not advance the campaign an inch, nor quicken a treaty of peace an hour, as the Mexicans universally regarded it as a mere border affair.

At the Brazos San Jago, I had to wait for the descent of the troops from Monterey, and also for the means of transportation to Vera Cruz. The general embarkation was thus unavoidably delayed till about February 15. At New Orleans I fortunately heard from old shipmasters that tolerable intermediate anchorage might be found in the terrible *northers*, behind the Lobos Islands—a group a third of the distance from Tampico toward Vera Cruz. Accordingly, I appointed that group as the general rendezvous for all the troop and supply ships of the expedition —many of them being still due from New Orleans and ports farther North.

Here, at the distance of some one hundred and twenty miles from Vera Cruz, I lay a few days with the van of the expedition, till the greater part of the troops and *matériel* of war expected had come up with me. Next we sailed a little past Vera Cruz and came to anchor, March 7, at Anton Lizardo, to take time for choosing, after reconnoissance, the best point of descent, to launch our boats and then to seize the first favorable state of the surf for debarkation—there being no harbor at or near the city. Ignorant of President Santa Anna's desperate march over the desert, upon Major-General Taylor, we did not doubt meeting at our landing the most formidable struggle of the war. No precaution therefore was neglected.

CHAPTER XXVIII.

SUCCESSFUL as was every prediction, plan, siege, battle, and skirmish of mine in the Mexican war, I have here paused many weeks to overcome the repugnance I feel to an entrance on the narrative of the campaign it was my fortune—I had almost said—*misfortune*—to conduct, with half means, beginning at Vera Cruz, March 9, and terminating in the capital of the country, September 14, 1847, six months and five days. This feeling is occasioned by the lively recollection of: 1. The perfidy of Mr. Polk; 2. The senseless and ungrateful clamor of Taylor, which, like his other prejudices, abided with him to the end;

3. The machinations of an ex-aide-de-camp—who owed his public *status* mainly to my helping hand; a vain man, of weak principles, and most inordinate ambition. The change commenced on learning that I had fallen under the ban at Washington; 4. The machinations of a Tennessee major-general, the special friend and partisan of Mr. Polk;—an anomaly,—without the least malignity in his nature—amiable, and possessed of some acuteness, but the only person I have ever known who was wholly indifferent in the choice between truth and falsehood, honesty and dishonesty;—ever as ready to attain an end by the one as the other, and habitually boastful of acts of cleverness at the total sacrifice of moral character. Procuring the nomination of Mr. Polk for the Presidency, he justly considered his greatest triumph in that way. These conspirators —for they soon coalesced—were joined by like characters—the first in time and malignity, a smart captain of artillery, whom they got brevetted, on brevet, more for the smoke of his guns than their shots, and to whom Mr. Polk, near the end of his term, gave the substantial reward of colonel and inspector-general,—an office that happened to fall vacant just then. "The ox knoweth his owner, and the ass his master's crib."

And alas, poor human nature! Even the brave Colonel Riley, the hero of Contreras (for which he was made a brigadier afterward), got the brevet of major-general and the command in California, by yielding to the same weakness. (See his testimony in the Pillow investigation.) These appointments proved an estate to Riley. The certainty of such fat benefits, freely promised by the conspirators, called into activity the sordid passions of other bribe-worthy officers. Hence the party of miscreants became quite respectable in numbers after the conquest. Those were not the only disgusts. The master outrage soon followed.

The offences of the two anonymous generals becoming a little too *prononcé*, I arrested both, and asked that a court might be ordered by the President for their trial. A court was ordered. I was relieved in the command, and the wronged and the wrong-doers, with stern impartiality! placed before the tribunal!! If I had lost the campaign it would have been difficult to heap upon me greater vexations and mortification.

May I add, that while I was before the court appointed by President Jackson, at Frederick, Maryland, Santa Anna passed by, and paid me, though I did not see him, an extravagant compliment? When he heard

18*

iu exile, that I was before a court at Mexico, he said to an American: "I thank President Polk—I am revenged!"

And why refer the appointment of a court to Washington? In 1830, Adjutant-General R. Jones was, on some slight occasion, arrested by the General-in-Chief, Macomb. The former had many friends in Congress, who ran a bill through the two Houses enacting that, when a commanding general arrests an officer or becomes the prosecutor of one, the court for the trial of the case shall be appointed by the President, etc. This provision being general, has caused a rent in the Administration of justice in the army, and ought to have been entitled *An Act to cripple generals commanding distant expeditions, and to unhinge the discipline* (subordination) *of armies.* Repeal is the only cure; but this error, it is feared, like universal suffrage, is a bourn from which there is no return. That it placed me, with such a President and such soldier demagogues, between the upper and nether millstones, must be perceived by all readers!

March 9—the precise day when I had been thirty years a general officer—the sun dawned propitiously on the expedition. There was but little surf on the beach

—a necessary condition—as we had to effect a landing from the open sea. Every detail, providing for all contingencies, had been discussed and arranged with my staff, and published in orders. The whole fleet of transports—some eighty vessels, in the presence of many foreign ships of war, stood up the coast, flanked by two naval steamers and five gunboats to cover the movement. Passing through them in the large propeller, the Massachusetts, the shouts and cheers from every deck gave me assurance of victory, whatever might be the force prepared to receive us.

We anchored opposite to a point a little beyond the range of the guns of the city and castle, when some fifty-five hundred men instantly filled up the sixty-seven surf boats I had caused to be built for this special occasion—each holding from seventy to eighty men—besides a few cutters belonging to the larger war vessels. Commodore Conner also supplied steerers (officers) and sailors as oarsmen. The whole, again cheering, as they passed my ship wearing the broad pennant, pulled away right for the shore, landed in the exact order prescribed, about half past five P. M., without the loss of a boat or a man, and, to the astonishment of all, without opposition other than a few whizzing shells that did no harm. Another trip or two enabled the row-boats to put ashore the whole force, rather less than twelve thousand men, though I had been promised double the number—my *minimum;* but I never had, at any one time in the campaign, more than thirteen thousand five hundred, until the fighting was over, when I was encumbered with the troops that Taylor found at last he could not use.

An article from the New Orleans *Bulletin*, of March 27, 1847, written by an intelligent pen, respecting the landing of troops, is here inserted :

" The landing of the American army at Vera Cruz has been accomplished in a manner that reflects the highest credit on all concerned ; and the regularity, precision, and promptness with which it was effected, has probably not been surpassed, if it has been equalled, in modern warfare.

" The removal of a large body of troops from numerous transports into boats in an open sea—their subsequent disembarkation on the sea-beach, on an enemy's coast, through a surf, with all their arms and accoutrements, without a single erro · or accident, requires great exertion, skill, and sound judgment.

" The French expedition against Algiers, in 1830, was said to be the most complete armament, in every respect, that ever left Europe; it had been prepared with labor, attention, and experience, and nothing had been omitted to insure success, and particularly in the means and facilities for landing the troops. This disembarkation took place in a wide bay, which was more favorable than an open beach directly on the ocean, and (as in the present instance) without any resistance on the part of the enemy—yet, only nine thousand men were landed the first day, and from thirty to forty lives were lost by accidents, or upsetting of boats; whereas, on the present occasion, twelve thousand men were landed in one day, without, so far as we have heard, the slightest accident, or the loss of a single life."

The city of Vera Cruz, and its castle, San Juan de Ulloa, were both strongly garrisoned. Santa Anna, relying upon them to hold out till the *vomito* (yellow fever) became rife, had returned to his capital, and was busy in collecting additional troops, mostly old, from every quarter of the republic, in order to crush the invasion, should it advance, at the first formidable pass in the interior.

The walls and forts of Vera Cruz, in 1847, were in good condition. Subsequent to its capture by the French under Admiral Baudin and Prince de Joinville, in 1838, the castle had been greatly extended—almost rebuilt, and its armament about doubled. Besides, the French were allowed to reconnoitre the city and castle, and choose their positions of attack without the least resistance—the Mexicans deprecating war with that nation, and hence ordered not to fire the first gun. Of that injunction the French were aware. When we approached, in 1847, the castle had the capacity to sink the entire American navy.

Immediately after landing, I made, with Colonel (soon after Brigadier-General) Totten, and other staff officers, a reconnoissance of the land side of the city, having previously reconnoitred the water front. This was at once followed by a close investment, so that there could be no communication between the garrisons and the interior. The blockade, by Commodore Conner, had long before been complete. Grave deliberations followed. From the first my hope had been to capture the castle under the shelter of, and through the city. This plan I had never submitted to discussion. Several Generals and Colonels—among them

Major-General Patterson—an excellent second in command, notwithstanding his failure as chief on the Shenandoah in 1861—solicited the privilege of leading storming parties. The applicants were thanked and applauded; but I forebore saying to them more. In my little cabinet, however, consisting of Colonel Totten, Chief Engineer, Lieutenant Colonel Hitchcock, acting Inspector-General, Captain R. E. Lee, Engineer, and (yet) First Lieutenant Henry L. Scott, acting Adjutant-General—I entered fully into the question of storming parties and regular siege approaches. A death-bed discussion could hardly have been more solemn. Thus powerfully impressed—feeling Mr. Polk's halter around my neck, as I expressed myself at the time—I opened the subject substantially as follows:

" We, of course, gentlemen, must take the city and castle before the return of the *vomito*—if not by headwork, the slow, scientific process, by storming—and then escape, by pushing the conquest into the healthy interior. I am strongly inclined to attempt the former unless you can convince me that the other is preferable. Since our thorough reconnoissance, I think the suggestion practicable with a very moderate loss on our part.

" The second method, would, no doubt, be equally successful, but at the cost of an immense slaughter to both sides, including non-combatants—Mexican men, women, and children—because assaults must be made in the dark, and the assailants dare not lose time in taking and guarding prisoners without incurring the certainty of becoming captives themselves, till all the strongholds of the place are occupied. The horrors of such slaughter, with the usual terrible accompaniments, are most revolting. Besides these objections, it is necessary to take into the account the probable loss of some two thousand, perhaps, three thousand of our best men in an assault, and I have received but half the numbers promised me. How then could we hope to penetrate the interior ? " " For these reasons," I added, quoting literally—" although I know our countrymen will hardly acknowledge a victory un-accompanied by a long butcher's bill (report of killed and wounded) I am strongly inclined—policy con-curring with humanity—to ' forego their loud applause and aves vehement,' and take the city with the least possible loss of life. In this determination I know, as Dogberry says truly of himself, I ' write me down an ass.' " *

My decided bias in favor of proceeding by siege, far from being combated, was fully concurred in. Accordingly Colonel Totten, the able chief engineer, and his accomplished assistants, proceeded to open the trenches and establish the batteries deemed necessary, after, by a general sweep, every post and sentry of the enemy had been driven in.

* When the victory of Buena Vista reached Major-General Brooke (a noble old soldier) commanding at New Orleans, and a friend of Major-General Taylor, he rushed, with the report in hand, through the streets to the Exchange, and threw the whole city into a frenzy of joy. By and by, came the news that the Stars and Stripes waved over Vera Cruz and its castle, and Brooke, also a friend of mine, was again eager to spread the report. Somebody in the crowd early called out : " How many men has Scott lost ? " Brooke was delighted to reply—" Less than a hundred." " That won't do," was promptly rejoined. " Taylor always loses thousands. He is the man for my money." Only a few faint cheers were heard for Vera Cruz. The long butcher's bill was wanted. When I received friend Brooke's letter giving these details, I own that my poor human nature was *piqued* for a moment; and I said: " Never mind. Taylor is a Louisianian. We shall, in due time, hear the voice of the Middle, the Northern, and Eastern States. They will estimate victories on different principles." But I was mistaken. The keynote raised in New Orleans was taken up all over the land. Mortifications are profitable to sufferers, and I record mine to teach aspirants to fame to cultivate humility; for blessed is the man who expects little, and can gracefully submit to less.

All sieges are much alike, and as this is not a treatise on engineering, scientific details are here omitted. We took care, in our approaches to keep the city as a shield between us and the terrible fire of the castle; but the forts in the walls of the city were formidable spitfires. They were rarely out of blast. Yet the approaches were so adroitly conducted, that our losses in them were surprisingly small, and no serious sortie was hazarded by the garrison.

The arming of the advanced batteries had been retarded by a very protracted gale (*norther*) which cut off all communication with our vessels in the offing. Ground was, however, broken on the 18th, and by the 22d, heavy ordnance enough for a beginning being in position, the governor of the city, who was also governor of the castle, was duly summoned to surrender. The refusal was no sooner received than a fire on the walls and forts was opened. In the attempt to batter in breach, and to silence the forts, a portion of our shots and shells, in the course of the siege, unavoidably penetrated the city and set fire to many houses. By the 24th, the landing of additional heavy guns and mortars gave us all the battering power needed, and the next day, as I reported to Washington, the whole was in " awful activity." The same day there came a memorial from the foreign consuls in Vera Cruz, asking for a truce to enable them, and the women and children of the inhabitants, to withdraw in safety. They had in time been duly warned of the impending danger, and allowed to the 22d to retire, which they had sullenly neglected, and the consuls had also declined the written *safe-guards* I had pressed upon them. The season had advanced, and I was aware of several cases of yellow fever in the city and neighborhood. Detachments of the enemy too were accumulating behind us, and rumors spread, by them, that a formidable army would soon approach to raise the siege. Tenderness therefore for the women and children—in the form of delay —might, in its consequences, have led to the loss of the campaign, and, indeed to the loss of the army—two thirds by pestilence, and the remainder by surrender. Hence I promptly replied to the consuls that no truce could be allowed except on the application of the governor (General Morales), and *that* with a view to surrender. Accordingly, the next morning General Landero, who had been put in the supreme command for that purpose, offered to entertain the question of submission. Commissioners were appointed on both sides, and on the 27th terms of surrender, including both the city and castle of Ulloa, agreed upon, signed and exchanged. The garrisons marched out, laying down their arms, and were sent home prisoners of war on parole.

This was better for the consuls, women, and children, as well as for the United States, than the *temporary* truce that I rejected—notwithstanding the ignorant censure cast on my conduct, on that occasion, by Mr. William Jay, in his book—*Review of the Causes and Consequences of the Mexican War*, pp. 202–4.

The surrender of the castle of San Juan de Ulloa, was necessarily involved in the fate of the city, because the enemy, until a late moment, had expected the former would be the first object of attack, and relying upon its impregnable strength, had neglected to lay in a supply of fresh water and provisions—as these could be sent over daily from the city. The capture of the latter, therefore, placed the castle entirely at our mercy.

The economy of life, by means of head-work, to which, as has been seen, Americans were quite indifferent, was never more conspicuous than on this occasion. The city and castle; the republic's principal port of foreign commerce; . five thousand prisoners, with a greater number of small arms;. four hundred pieces of ordnance and large stores of ammunition, were the great results of the first twenty days after our landing, and all at the very small loss, in numbers, of sixty-four officers and men killed or wounded. Among the slain were two captains, J. R. Vinton and W. Alburtis, both of high merit—Vinton, perhaps, the most accomplished officer in the army. The enemy's loss in killed and wounded was not considerable, and of other persons—citizens—not three were slain—all being in stone houses, and most of the inhabitants taking refuge in basements.

The official report of those extraordinary successes, in which due praise was bestowed on corps and officers by name, as well as on the coöperation of the navy, was taken to Washington by Colonel Totten, of the Engineers, who was duly brevetted a brigadier-general for his great services in the siege.

CHAPTER XXIX.

BATTLE OF CERRO GORDO, JALAPA, PEROTE AND PUEBLA
—HALTS—VISIT TO CHOLULA.

FORTUNATELY, the frequency of the gales, called *northers*, had kept off the *vomito*, as an epidemic, though a few cases had occurred in the city ; but, unfortunately, the want of road-power—horses and mules—detained the body of the army at Vera Cruz from its capture, March 29, till toward the middle of April.

Some wagons and harness came first, and by the 8th, we hitched up a train sufficient to put Brigadier-General Twiggs's division, composed of brigades under Colonels Harney and Riley, with Major Talcott's light battery, all regulars, in march for the interior. Major-General Patterson, commanding a division of three volunteer brigades, under Brigadier-Generals Pillow, Quitman, and Shields, was next supplied with partial means of transportation, and followed Twiggs. Draft animals and wagons continued to arrive slowly (more of the latter than the former), but never in sufficient numbers. Hence a siege train of six pieces only, four of which were heavy, was fitted for the road, and hence Worth's division of regulars was detained until the 16th. Each division and detachment of troops had instructions to take, in wagons, subsistence for men equal to six days, and oats for horses equal to three, besides the usual number of cooked rations for men in haversacks.

Those supplies were deemed indispensable to take the corps to Jalapa, a productive region, abounding in many articles of food as well as in mules, which we so much needed for the remaining wagons at Vera Cruz. Some hundreds of these animals were purchased, and sent below to bring up ammunition, medicines, hospital stores, clothing, and some bacon, there being but little in the country, and fresh beef not always to be had. But this is anticipating.

Hearing that Twiggs, supported by Patterson, found himself confronted at Plan del Rio, some fifty miles in the interior, by a strong body of the enemy, and that both divisions were desirous of my presence, I left Vera Cruz on the 12th of April, with a small escort of cavalry under Captain Philip Kearny (who fell in 1862, a distinguished major-general), and hastened to the front. Major-General Patterson, though quite sick, had assumed the command on joining Twiggs, in order to prohibit any aggressive movement before my arrival, according to the universal wish of the troops. No commander was ever received with heartier cheers—the certain presage of the victories that followed.

The two advanced divisions lay in the valley of the Plan del Rio, and the body of the enemy about three miles off, on the heights of Cerro Gordo. Reconnaissances were pushed in search of some practicable route, other than the winding, zig-zag road, among the spurs of mountains, with heavy batteries at every turn. The reconanissances were conducted with vigor under Captain Lee, at the head of a body of pioneers, and at the end of the third day, a passable way for light batteries was accomplished—without alarming the enemy—giving the possibility of turning the extreme left of liis line of defences, and capturing his whole army, except the reserve that lay a mile or two higher up the road.

Santa Anna said, after the event, that he had not believed a goat could have approached him in that direction. Hence the surprise and results were the greater.

The time for aggression being at hand, I—in order to insure harmony by letting all commanders know what each was expected to execute—issued this prophetic order:

GENERAL ORDERS, }
No. 111.

HEADQUARTERS OF THE ARMY,
PLAN DEL RIO, *April* 17, 1847.

The enemy's whole line of intrenchments and batteries will be attacked in front, and at the same time turned, early in the day to-morrow—probably before ten o'clock A. M.

The second (Twiggs's) division of regulars is already advanced within easy turning distance toward the enemy's left. That division has instructions to move forward before daylight to-morrow, and take up position across the national road in the enemy's rear, so as to cut off a retreat toward Jalapa. It may be reënforced to-day, if unexpectedly attacked in force, by regiments—one or two—taken from Shields's brigade of volunteers. If not, the two volunteer regiments will

19

march for that purpose at daylight to-morrow morning, under Brigadier-General Shields, who will report to Brigadier-General Twiggs on getting up with him, or to the general-in-chief, if he be in advance.

The remaining regiment of that volunteer brigade will receive instructions in the course of this day.

The first division of regulars (Worth's) will follow the movement against the enemy's left at sunrise to-morrow morning.

As already arranged, Brigadier-General Pillow's brigade will march at six o'clock to-morrow morning, along the route he has carefully reconnoitred, and stand ready, as soon as he hears the report of arms on our right, or sooner, if circumstances should favor him, to pierce the enemy's line of batteries at such point—the nearer to the river the better—as he may select. Once in the rear of that line, he will turn to the right or left, or both, and attack the batteries in reverse, or, if abandoned, he will pursue the enemy with vigor until further orders.

Wall's field battery and the cavalry will be held in reserve on the national road, a little out of view and range of the enemy's batteries. They will take up that position at nine o'clock in the morning.

The enemy's batteries being carried or abandoned, all our divisions and corps will pursue with vigor.

This pursuit may be continued many miles, until stopped by darkness or fortified positions, toward Jalapa. Consequently, the body of the army will not return to this encampment; but be followed, to-morrow afternoon or early the next morning, by the baggage trains of the several corps. For this purpose, the feebler officers and men of each corps will be left to guard its camp and effects, and to load up the latter in the wagons of the corps. A commander of the present encampment will be designated in the course of this day.

As soon as it shall be known that the enemy's works have been carried, or that the general pursuit has been commenced, one wagon for each regiment and battery, and one for the cavalry, will follow the movement, to receive, under the direction of medical officers, the wounded and disabled, who will be brought back to this place for treatment in general hospital.

The surgeon-general will organize this important service, and designate that hospital as well as the medical officers to be left at it.

Every man who marches out to attack or pursue

the enemy will take the usual allowance of ammunition, and subsistence for at least two days.

By command of Major-General Scott.

II. L. SCOTT,

A. A.-General.

Headquartes of the Army, Plan
del Rio, Fifty Miles from
Vera Cruz, *April* 19, 1847.

Sir:

The plan of attack, sketched in General Orders No. 111, herewith, was finely executed by this gallant army before two o'clock p. m., yesterday. We are quite embarrassed with the results of victory—prisoners of war, heavy ordnance, field batteries, small arms, and accoutrements. About 3,000 men laid down their arms, with the usual proportion of field and company officers, besides five generals, several of them of great distinction—Pinson, Jarrero, La Vega, Noriega, and Obando. A sixth general, Vasquez, was killed in defending the battery (tower) in the rear of the line of defence, the capture of which gave us those glorious results.

Our loss, though comparatively small in numbers,

has been serious. Brigadier-General Shields, a commander of activity, zeal, and talent, is, I fear, if not dead, mortally wounded. He is some five miles from me at the moment. The field of operations covered many miles, broken by mountains and deep chasms, and I have not a report as yet from any division or brigade. Twiggs's division, followed by Shields's (now Colonel Baker's) brigade, are now at or near Jalapa, and Worth's division is in route thither; all pursuing, with good results, as I learn, that part of the Mexican army, perhaps six or seven thousand men, that fled before our right had carried the tower, and gained the Jalapa road. Pillow's brigade alone is near me at this depot of wounded, sick, and prisoners, and I have time only to give from him the names of First Lieutenant F. B. Nelson, and Second Lieutenant C. G. Gill, both of the 2d Tennessee Foot (Haskell's regiment), among the killed; and in the brigade, one hundred and six of all ranks killed or wounded. Among the latter, the gallant Brigadier-General himself has a smart wound in the arm, but not disabled, and Major R. Farqueson, 2d Tennessee; Captain H. F. Murray, Second Lieutenant G. T. Sutherland, First Lieutenant W. P. Hale (Adjutant), all of the same regiment, severely, and First Lieutenant W. Yearwood, mortally wounded. And I know, from personal observation on the ground, that First Lieutenant Ewell, of the Rifles, if not now dead, was mortally wounded in entering, sword in hand, the intrenchments around the captured tower. Second Lieutenant Derby, Topographical Engineers, I also saw, at the same place, severely wounded, and Captain Patten, 2d United States' Infantry, lost his right hand. Major Sumner, 2d United States' Dragoons, was slightly wounded the day before, and Captain Johnston, Topographical Engineers (now Lieutenant-Colonel of infantry), was very severely wounded, some days earlier, while reconnoitring. I must not omit to add that Captain Mason and Second Lieutenant Davis, both of the Rifles, were among the very severely wounded in storming the same tower. I estimate our total loss in killed and wounded may be about two hundred and fifty, and that of the enemy three hundred and fifty. In the pursuit toward Jalapa (twenty-five miles hence), I learn we have added much to the enemy's loss in prisoners, killed, and wounded. In fact, I suppose his retreating army to be nearly disorganized; and hence my haste to follow, in an hour or two, to profit by events.

In this hurried and imperfect report I must not omit to say that Brigadier-General Twiggs, in passing the mountain range beyond Cerro Gordo, crowned with the tower, detached from his division, as I suggested the day before, a strong force to carry that height, which commanded the Jalapa road at the foot, and could not fail, if carried, to cut off the whole or any part of the enemy's forces from a retreat in any direction. A portion of the 1st Artillery, under the often distinguished Brevet Colonel Childs, the 3d Infantry, under Captain Alexander, the 7th Infantry, under Lieutenant-Colonel Plympton, and the Rifles, under Major Loring, all under the temporary command of Colonel Harney, 2d Dragoons, during the confinement to his bed of Brevet Brigadier-General P. F. Smith, composed that detachment. The style of execution, which I had the pleasure to witness, was most brilliant and decisive. The brigade ascended the long and difficult slope of Cerro Gordo, without shelter, and under the tremendous fire of artillery and musketry, with the utmost steadiness, reached the breastworks, drove the enemy from them, planted the colors of the 1st Artillery, 3d and 7th Infantry—the enemy's flag still flying—and after some minutes of sharp firing, finished the conquest with the bayonet.

It is a most pleasing duty to say that the highest praise is due to Harney, Childs, Plympton, Loring, Alexander, their gallant officers and men, for this brilliant service, independent of the great results which soon followed.

Worth's division of regulars coming up at this time, he detached Brevet Lieutenant-Colonel C. F. Smith, with his light battalion, to support the assault, but not in time. The general, reaching the tower a few minutes before me, and observing a white flag displayed from the nearest portion of the enemy toward the batteries below, sent out Colonels Harney and Childs to hold a parley. The surrender followed in an hour or two.

Major-General Patterson left a sickbed to share in the dangers and fatigues of the day; and after the surrender went forward to command the advanced forces toward Jalapa.

Brigadier-General Pillow and his brigade twice assaulted with great daring the enemy's line of batteries on our left; and, though without success, they contributed much to distract and dismay their immediate opponents.

President Santa Anna, with Generals Canalizo and Ampudia, and some six or eight thousand men, escaped toward Jalapa just before Cerro Gordo was carried, and before Twiggs's division reached the national road above.

I have determined to parole the prisoners—officers and men—as I have not the means of feeding them here beyond to-day, and cannot afford to detach a heavy body of horse and foot, with wagons, to accompany them to Vera Cruz. Our baggage train, though increasing, is not yet half large enough to give an assured progress to this army. Besides, a greater number of prisoners would probably escape from the escort in the long and deep sandy road without subsistence— ten to one—than we shall find again out of the same body of men in the ranks opposed to us. Not one of the Vera Cruz prisoners is believed to have been in the lines of Cerro Gordo. Some six of the officers, highest in rank, refuse to give their paroles, except to go to Vera Cruz, and thence, perhaps, to the United States.

The small arms and their accoutrements, being of no value to our army here or at home, I have ordered them to be destroyed; for we have not the means of transporting them. I am also somewhat embarrassed

19*

with the —— pieces of artillery—all bronze—which we have captured. It would take a brigade and half the mules of this army to transport them fifty miles. A field battery I shall take for service with the army; but the heavy metal must be collected and left here for the present. We have our own siege-train and the proper carriages with us.

Being much occupied with the prisoners and all the details of a forward movement, besides looking to the supplies which are to follow from Vera Cruz, I have time to add no more—intending to be at Jalapa early to-morrow. We shall not probably again meet with serious opposition this side of Perote—certainly not, unless delayed by the want of the means of transportation.

I have the honor to remain, sir, with high respect, your most obedient servant,

WINFIELD SCOTT.

P. S.—I invite attention to the accompanying letter to President Santa Anna, taken in his carriage yesterday; also to his proclamation, issued on hearing that we had captured Vera Cruz, etc., in which he says: "If the enemy advance one step more, the national

independence will be buried in the abyss of the past."
We have taken that step.

W: S.

I make a second postscript, to say there is some
hope, I am happy to learn, that General Shields may
survive his wounds.

One of the principal motives for paroling the prisoners of war is to diminish the resistance of other garrisons in our march.

W. S.

Hon. Wm. L. Marcy, *Secretary of War.*

Headquarters of the Army,
Jalapa, *April* 23, 1847.

Sir:

In forwarding the reports of commanders which
detail the operations of their several corps against the
Mexican lines at Cerro Gordo, I shall present, in continuation of my former report, but an outline of the
affair, and while adopting heartily their commendations of the ardor and efficiency of individuals, I shall
mention by name only those who figure prominently,

or, from position, could not be included in those sub-
reports.

The field sketch herewith, indicates the positions
of the two armies. The *tierra caliente*, or low level,
terminates at *Plan del Rio*, the site of the American
camp, from which the road ascends immediately in a
long circuit among lofty hills, whose commanding
points had all been fortified and garrisoned by the
enemy. His right, intrenched, rested on a precipice
overhanging an impassable ravine that forms the bed
of the stream; and his intrenchments extended con-
tinuously to the road, on which was placed a formidable battery. On the other side, the lofty and difficult
height of Cerro Gordo commanded the approaches in
all directions. The main body of the Mexican army
was encamped on level ground, with a battery of five
pieces, half a mile in rear of that height toward Jalapa.

Resolving, if possible, to turn the enemy's left, and
attack in rear, while menacing or engaging his front, I
caused daily reconnaissances to be pushed, with the
view of finding a route for a force to debouch on the
Jalapa road and cut off retreat.

The reconnaissance begun by Lieutenant Beauregard, was continued by Captain Lee, Engineers, and a

road made along difficult slopes and over chasms—out of the enemy's view, though reached by his fire when discovered—until, arriving at the Mexican lines, further reconnaissance became impossible without an action. The desired point of debouchure, the Jalapa road, was not therefore reached, though believed to be within easy distance; and to gain that point, it now became necessary to carry the height of Cerro Gordo. The dispositions in my plan of battle—general orders No. 111, heretofore enclosed—were accordingly made.

Twiggs's division, reënforced by Shields's brigade of volunteers, was thrown into position on the 17th, and was, of necessity, drawn into action in taking up the ground for its bivouac and the opposing height for our heavy battery. It will be seen that many of our officers and men were killed or wounded in this sharp combat—handsomely commenced by a company of the 7th Infantry under Brevet First Lieutenant Gardner, who is highly praised by all his commanders for signal services. Colonel Harney coming up with the rifle regiment and 1st Artillery (also parts of his brigade) brushed away the enemy and occupied the height—on which, in the night, was placed a battery of one 24-pounder and two 24-pound howitzers, under the superintendence of Captain Lee, Engineers, and Lieutenant Hagner, Ordnance. These guns opened next morning, and were served with effect by Captain Steptoe and Lieutenant Brown, 3d Artillery, Lieutenant Hagner (Ordnance), and Lieutenant Seymour, 1st Artillery.

The same night, with extreme toil and difficulty, under the superintendence of Lieutenant Tower, Engineer, and Lieutenant Laidley, Ordnance, an eight-inch howitzer was put in position across the river and opposite to the enemy's right battery. A detachment of four companies, under Major Burnham, New York Volunteers, performed this creditable service, which enabled Lieutenant Ripley, 2d Artillery, in charge of the piece, to open a timely fire in that quarter.

Early on the 18th, the columns moved to the general attack, and our success was speedy and decisive. Pillow's brigade, assaulting the right of the intrenchments, although compelled to retire, had the effect I have heretofore stated. Twiggs's division, storming the strong and vital point of Cerro Gordo, pierced the centre, gained command of all of the intrenchments, and cut them off from support. As our infantry (Colonel Riley's brigade) pushed on against the main body of the enemy, the guns of their own fort were rapidly turned to play on that force (under the immediate command of General Santa Anna), who fled in confusion. Shields's brigade, bravely assaulting the left, carried the rear battery (five guns) on the Jalapa road, and aided materially in completing the rout of the enemy.

The part taken by the remainder of our forces, held in reserve to support and pursue, has already been noticed.

The moment the fate of the day was decided, the cavalry, and Taylor's, and Wall's field batteries were pushed on toward Jalapa in advance of the pursuing columns of infantry—Twiggs's division and the Brigade of Shields (now under Colonel Baker)—and Major-General Patterson was sent to take command of them. In the hot pursuit many Mexicans were captured or slain before our men and horses were exhausted by the heat and distance.

The rout proves to have been complete—the retreating army, except a small body of cavalry, being dispersed and utterly disorganized. The immediate consequences have been our possession of this important city, the abandonment of the works and artillery at La Hoya, the next formidable pass between Vera Cruz and the capital, and the prompt occupation by Worth's division of the fortress of Perote (second only to San Juan de Ulloa), with its extensive armament of sixty-six guns and mortars, and its large supplies of *matériel.* To General Worth's report, annexed, I refer for details.

I have heretofore endeavored to do justice to the skill and courage with which the attack on the height of Cerro Gordo was directed and executed, naming the regiments most distinguished, and their commanders, under the lead of Colonel Harney. Lieutenant G. W. Smith led the engineer company as part of the storming force, and is noticed with distinction.

The reports of this assault make favorable mention of many in which I can well concur, having witnessed the daring advance and perfect steadiness of the whole. Beside those already named, Lieutenant Brooks, 3d Infantry; Lieutenant Macdonald, 2d Dragoons; Lieutenant Vandorn, 7th Infantry—all acting staff officers—Captain Magruder, 1st Artillery, and Lieutenant Gardner, 7th Infantry, seem to have won especial praise.

Colonel Riley's brigade and Talcott's rocket and howitzer battery, were engaged on and about the heights, and bore an active part.

The brigade so gallantly led by General Shields, and, after his fall, by Colonel Baker, deserves high commendation for its fine behavior and success. Colonels Foreman and Burnett, and Major Harris, commanded the regiments; Lieutenant Hammond, 3d Artillery, and Lieutenant Davis, Illinois Volunteers, constituted the brigade staff. These operations, hid from my view by intervening hills, were not fully known when my first report was hastily written.

Brigadier-General Twiggs, who was in the immediate command of all the advanced forces, has earned high credit by his judgment, spirit, and energy.

The conduct of Colonels Campbell, Haskell, and Wynkoop, commanding the regiments of Pillow's brigade, is reported in terms of strong approbation by Major-General Patterson. I recommend for a commission, Quartermaster-Sergeant Henry, of the 7th Infantry (already known to the army for intrepidity on former occasions), who hauled down the national standard of the Mexican fort.

In expressing my indebtedness for able assistance to Lieutenant-Colonel Hitchcock, Acting Inspector-General, to Majors Smith and Turnbull, the respective Chiefs of Engineers and Topographical Engineers—

to their Assistants, Lieutenants Mason, Beauregard, Stevens, Tower, G. W. Smith, McClellan, Engineers, and Lieutenants Derby and Hardcastle, Topographical Engineers—to Captain Allen, Chief Quartermaster, and Lieutenant Blair, Chief Commissary—and to Lieutenants Hagner and Laidley, Ordnance—all actively employed—I am compelled to make special mention of the services of Captain R. E. Lee, Engineer. This officer, greatly distinguished at the siege of Vera Cruz, was again indefatigable, during these operations, in reconnaissances as daring as laborious, and of the utmost value. Nor was he less conspicuous in planting batteries, and in conducting columns to their stations under the heavy fire of the enemy.

My personal staff, Lieutenants Scott, Williams, and Lay, and Major Van Buren, who volunteered for the occasion, gave me zealous and efficient assistance.

Our whole force present, in action and in reserve, was eight thousand five hundred; the enemy is estimated at twelve thousand, or more. About three thousand prisoners, four or five thousand stands of arms, and forty-three pieces of artillery were taken. By the accompanying return, I regret to find our loss more severe than at first supposed, amounting in the two days to thirty-three officers and three hundred and ninety-eight men—in all four hundred and thirty-one, of whom sixty-three were killed. The enemy's loss is computed to be from one thousand to one thousand two hundred.

I am happy in communicating strong hopes of the recovery of.the gallant General Shields, who is so much improved as to have been brought to this place.

Appended to this report are the following papers:

A.—General return by name of killed and wounded.

B.—Copies of report of Lieutenant-Colonel Hitch-cock, Acting Inspector-General (of prisoners taken) and accompanying papers.

C.—Report of Brigadier-General Twiggs, and sub-reports.

D.—Report of Major-General Patterson, and reports of brigade commanders.

E.—Copy of report of.Brigadier-General Worth, announcing the occupation by his division of the castle and town of Perote, without opposition with an inventory of ordnance there found.

I have the honor to remain, sir, with high respect, your most obedient servant,

WINFIELD SCOTT.

Hon. Wm. L. Marcy, *Secretary of War.*

This terrible blow following closely on the captures of the preceding month, threw the Mexicans into consternation. Jalapa was abandoned, and I pushed Worth's division forward to tread on the heels of the fugitives and increase the panic.

Approaching Perote, its formidable castle also opened its gates without firing a gun, and the same division took quiet possession of the great city of Puebla. But here the career of conquest was arrested for a time.

I had been obliged to lessen the strength of a diminutive army by leaving respectable garrisons of regulars, in Vera Cruz and the Castle of San Juan de Ulloa. And now at Jalapa, without having received any reënforcements, it became necessary to discharge some four thousand volunteers whose respective terms of service were about to expire. They gave notice that they would continue with me to the last day, but would then certainly demand discharges and the means of transportation homeward. As any delay might throw them upon the yellow fever, at Vera Cruz, the discharges were given at once.

We were delayed nearly a month at Jalapa waiting for a partial supply of necessaries from Vera Cruz by the second and third trips of our feeble trains, and with a faint hope of reënforcements. Not a company came. At length, toward the end of May, I marched, with the reserve, to join the advanced division (Worth's) at Puebla—leaving a strong garrison at Jalapa, under Colonel Childs, to keep the line of communication open with Vera Cruz as long as possible. Indeed, at that time, I had not entirely lost the hope of receiving new regiments of regulars and volunteers in numbers sufficient to maintain our communications with the ocean and home throughout the campaign by means of garrisons at the National Bridge, Perote, Puebla, and Rio Frio, as well as at Vera Cruz and Jalapa.

Waiting for reënforcements, the halt, at Puebla, was protracted and irksome. The Benton intrigue had so disgusted a majority of the two houses of Congress, that the bill authorizing the ten new regiments of regulars lingered from the beginning of December down to the 11th of February—the Administration having sunk too low to hasten its passage a day in advance of the usual sluggish forms of legislation.

In the mean time, the army at Puebla was not inactive. All the corps, amounting to about five thousand effective men, were daily put through their manœuvres and evolutions. We were also kept on the alert by an army sometimes of superior numbers, hovering about us, and often assuming a menacing attitude; but always ready for flight the moment they saw that we were under arms. On these occasions it was painful to restrain the ardor of the troops. But I steadily held to the policy not to wear out patience and sole leather by running to the right or left in the pursuit of small game. I played for the big stakes. Keeping the army massed and the mind fixed upon the capital, I meant to content myself with beating whatever force that might stand directly in the way of that conquest—being morally sure that all smaller objects would soon follow that crowning event.

The city of Puebla, washed by a fine, flowing stream, is near the centre of a valley of uncommon fertility and beauty, producing, annually, two abundant crops for the subsistence of men and animals—one by rains, and the other by artificial irrigation. All the cereals—wheat, barley, maize and rye; all the grasses, including clover, lucerne, and timothy, and all the fruit-trees—the apple, peach, apricot and pear, grow here as well as in the region of Frederic, Maryland—the elevation (near seven thousand feet above the ocean) making a difference in climate, equal to eighteen or twenty degrees of latitude. Many objects within the horizon of Puebla are among the sublimest features of nature. The white peak of Orizaba, the most distant, may always be seen in bright weather. The Malinche mountain, near by, is generally capped with snow; Popocatapetl and his white sister, always, since the first snow fell after the creation. The city itself, with her hundred steeples and cathedral, in majestic repose—seen from a certain elevation, is itself a magnificent object in the gerreral landscape.

During this halt, every corps of the army in succession, made a most interesting excursion of six miles, to the ruins of the ancient city of Cholula, long, in point of civilization and art, the Etruria of this continent, and in respect to religion, the Mecca of many of the earliest tribes known to tradition. Down to the time of Cortes, a little more than three hundred years before the Americans, Cholula, containing an ingenious and peaceable population of perhaps one hundred and fifty thousand souls, impressed with a *unique* type of civilization, had fallen off, in 1847, to a miserable hamlet, its towers and dwellings of sun-baked bricks and stucco, in heaps of ruins. From these melancholy wrecks are yet disinterred productions of art of great beauty and delicacy, in metals and porcelain, both for ornament and use. The same people also manufactured cloths of cotton and the fibre of the agave plant.

One grand feature, denoting the ancient grandeur of Cholula, stands but little affected by the lapse of perhaps thousands of years—a pyramid built of alternate layers of brick and clay, some two hundred feet in height, with a square basis of more than forty acres, running up to a plateau of seventy yards square. There stood in the time of Cortes, the great pagan temple of the Cholulans, with a perpetual blazing fire on its altar, seen in the night many miles around. This the Spaniards soon replaced by a *bijou* of a church, something larger than the *Casa Santa* at Loretto, with a beautiful altar and many pictures. The ascent to this plateau is by a flight of some hundred and forty steps.

The prosperity of Cholula, in 1520, was already on the decline, having recently fallen under the harsh rule of the Montezumas, and it now sustained a heavy blow at the hands of Cortes, an invited guest, who, to punish a detected conspiracy, that was intended to compass the destruction of his entire army, massacred more than six thousand of the inhabitants, including most of the chiefs, besides destroying entire streets of houses.

An admirer of scenery, and curious to view the ruins of Cholula, the autobiographer, one bright morning in June, suddenly determined to overtake a fine brigade of regulars that had advanced on that excursion, half an hour before. Even escorted by a squadron of cavalry this was an enterprise not without some danger, considering that he could make no movement without causing several citizens to fly off at full speed, on fine Andalusian horses, to report the fact to detachments of cavalry lurking in the vicinity.

Coming up with the brigade marching at ease,* all intoxicated with the fine air and splendid scenery, he was, as usual, received with hearty and protracted cheers. The group of officers who surrounded him, differed widely in the objects of their admiration— some preferring this or that snow-capped mountain, others the city, and several the pyramid of Cholula, that was now opening upon the view. An appeal from all was made to the general-in-chief. He emphatically replied : "I differ from you all. My greatest

* Troops, marching at ease, bear their arms on either shoulder or in either hand, always keeping the muzzles of their arms up, and are at liberty to talk, laugh, sing or crack their jokes to their heart's content—only taking care not to confound their ranks.

delight is in this fine body of troops, without whom,
we can never sleep in the Halls of the Montezumas, or
in our own homes." The word was caught up by some
of the rank and file, marching abreast, and passed
rapidly to the front and rear of the column, each
platoon, in succession, rending the air with its accla-
mation.

CHAPTER XXX.

At length reënforcements began to approach.
Lieutenant-Colonel McIntosh with some eight hundred
men, escorting a large train, was checked and delayed
by the enemy in the march near Jalapa; but being
soon joined by Brigadier-General Cadwallader, with a
portion of his brigade and a field battery, the enemy
was swept away and the two detachments arrived in
safety at Puebla. Major-General Pillow followed with
another detachment of a thousand men, and finally
came Brigadier-General Pierce (August the 6th) with
a brigade of two thousand five hundred.

About this time, when General Taylor had more troops than he could employ, and yet clamored for re-enforcements—I was obliged, by paucity of numbers, to call up the garrison from Jalapa, under Colonel Childs, to make up my entire force at Puebla including the late reënforcements, to about fourteen thousand men, of whom two thousand five hundred were sick in hospital (mostly diarrhœa cases), and about six hundred convalescents, yet too feeble for an ordinary day's march. The latter, and an equal number of effective troops were designated as the garrison, under Colonel Childs, of the important city of Puebla—the whole route to Vera Cruz and all communications with home, being, for the time, abandoned. We had to throw away the scabbard and to advance with the naked blade in hand.

The composition of the army in its march from Puebla to Mexico was as follows:

GENERAL STAFF.

Lieutenant-Colonel Hitchcock, Assistant Inspector-General.
Captain H. L. Scott, Acting Adjutant-General.
First Lieutenant T. Williams, Aide-de-Camp.
Brevet First Lieutenant G. W. Lay, Aide-de-Camp.

Second Lieutenant Schuyler Hamilton, Aide-de-Camp.
Major J. P. Gaines, Volunteer Aide-de-Camp.

ENGINEER CORPS.

Major J. L. Smith, Chief.
Captain R. E. Lee.
Lieutenant P. G. T. Beauregard.
  " Isaac I. Stevens.
  " Z. B. Tower.
  " G. W. Smith.
  " George B. McClellan.
  " J. G. Foster.

ORDNANCE DEPARTMENT.

Captain Benjamin Huger, Chief, with Siege Train.
First Lieutenant P. V. Hagner.
Second Lieutenant C. P. Stone.

TOPOGRAPHICAL ENGINEERS.

Major William Turnbull, Chief.
Captain J. McClellan.
Second Lieutenant George Thom.
Brevet Second Lieutenant E. L. F. Hardcastle.

QUARTERMASTER'S DEPARTMENT.

Captain J. R. Irwin, Chief.
  " A. C. Myers.
  " Robert Allen.
  " H. C. Wayne.
  " J. McKinstry.
  " G. W. F. Wood.

Captain J. Daniels.
    "   O'Hara.
    "   S. McGowan.

SUBSISTENCE DEPARTMENT.

Captain J. B. Grayson, Chief.
    "   T. P. Randle.

PAY DEPARTMENT.

Major E. Kirby, Chief.
    "   A. Van Buren.
    "   A. G. Bennett.

MEDICAL DEPARTMENT.

Surgeon-General Thomas Lawson.
Surgeon B. F. Harney.
    "   R. S. Satterlee.
    "   C. S. Tripler.
    "   B. Randall.
    "   J. M. Cuyler.
Assistant-Surgeon A. F Suter.
    "   "   J. Simpson.
    "   "   D. C. DeLeon.
    "   "   H. H. Steiner.
    "   "   J. Simons.
    "   "   J. K. Barnes.
    "   "   L. H. Holden.
    "   "   C. C. Keeney.
    "   "   J. F. Head.
    "   "   J. F. Hammond.
    "   "   J. M. Steiner.

Assistant-Surgeon C. P. Deyerle.
    "   "   E. Swift.
Surgeon J. M. Tyler,   Volunteer.
    "   McMillan,   "
    "   C. J. Clark,   "
    "   W. B. Halstead,   "
Assistant-Surgeon R. Hagan,   Volunteer.
    "   "   H. L. Wheaton,   "
Surgeon R. Ritchie, 1st Volunteers.
    "   J. Barry,   "
    "   Edwards,   "
    "   L. W. Jordan,   "
    "   R. McSherry,   "
    "   Roberts,   "

CORPS.

COLONEL HARNEY'S BRIGADE.

Detachment of 1st Light Dragoons, under Captain Kearny.
    "   2d   "   " Major Sumner.
    "   3d   "   " Major McReynolds.

I.—BREVET MAJOR-GENERAL WORTH'S DIVISION.

1. COLONEL GARLAND'S BRIGADE.

2d Regiment of Artillery, serving as Infantry.
3d   "   "   "   "
4th   "   of Infantry.
Duncan's Field Battery.

2. COLONEL CLARK'S BRIGADE.

5th, 6th and 8th Regiments of Infantry.
A Light Battery.

II.—BREVET MAJOR-GENERAL TWIGGS'S DIVISION.

1. BREVET BRIGADIER-GENERAL P. F. SMITH'S BRIGADE.

Rifle Regiment.
1st Regiment of Artillery, serving as Infantry.
3d Regiment of Infantry.
Taylor's Light Battery.

2. COLONEL RILEY'S BRIGADE.

4th Regiment of Artillery, serving as Infantry.
1st Regiment of Infantry.
7th   "   "

III.—MAJOR-GENERAL PILLOW'S DIVISION.

1. BRIGADIER-GENERAL G. CADWALLADER'S BRIGADE.

Voltigeurs.
11th and 14th Infantry.
A Light Battery.

2. BRIGADIER-GENERAL PIERCE'S BRIGADE.

9th, 12th, and 15th Infantry.

IV.—MAJOR-GENERAL QUITMAN'S DIVISION.

1. BRIGADIER-GENERAL SHIELDS'S BRIGADE.

New York Volunteers.
South Carolina Volunteers.

2. LIEUTENANT-COLONEL WATSON'S BRIGADE.

A Detachment of 2d Pennsylvania Volunteers.
Detachment of United States' Marines.

It has been seen that the last body of recruits (Pierce's brigade) arrived August 6, 1847. The army commenced its advance, by divisions, on the 7th— Twiggs's division first, with Harney's brigade of cavalry leading, and the siege train following. The other three divisions successively followed on the 8th, 9th, and 10th—each of the four divisions making but a half day's march at the beginning. So that no division (even the leading or rearmost one) was ever separated more than seven or eight miles from support, or rather half that distance, by means of a double movement— one division advancing and the other falling back. By similar means, three divisions might easily have been united in little more than two hours, in the case of a formidable attack upon an interior division.

20*

This concatenation of the advancing corps was deemed prudent inasmuch as President Santa Anna had now had nearly four months (since the battle of Cerro Gordo) to collect and reorganize the entire means of the Republic for a last vigorous attempt to crush the invasion. A single error on our part—a single victory on his, might have effected that great end.* His vigilance and energy were unquestionable, and his powers of creating and organizing worthy of admiration. He was also great in administrative ability, and though not deficient in personal courage, he, on the field of battle, failed in quickness of perception and rapidity of combination. Hence his defeats.

We had confidently expected to meet him, at the latest, in the defiles of Rio Frio; but he preferred remaining in coil about the city in the midst of formidable lines of defence both natural and artificial.

August 10, the leading division, with which I marched, crossed the Rio Frio range of mountains, the

---

* The Duke of Wellington, with whom the autobiographer was slightly acquainted, took quite an interest in the march of this army from Vera Cruz, and at every arrival caused its movements to be marked on a map. Admiring its triumphs up to the basin of Mexico, he now said to a common friend: " Scott is lost. He has been carried away by successes. He can't take the city, and he can't fall back upon his base."

highest point, in the bed of the road between the Atlántic and Pacific Oceans.

Descending the long western slope, a magnificent basin, with, near its centre, the object of all our dreams and hopes—toils and dangers;—once the gorgeous seat of the Montezumas, now the capital of a great Republic—first broke upon our enchanted view. The close surrounding lakes, sparkling under a bright sun, seemed, in the distance, pendant diamonds. The numerous steeples of great beauty and elevation, with Popocatepetl, ten thousand feet higher, apparently near enough to touch with the hand, filled the mind with religious awe. Recovering from the sublime trance, probably, not a man in the column failed to say to his neighbor or himself: *That splendid city soon shall be ours!* All were ready to suit the action to the word.

Report No. 31.

HEADQUARTERS OF THE ARMY, SAN AUGUSTIN, ACAPULCO ROAD, NINE MILES FROM MEXICO, *August* 19, 1847.

SIR:

Leaving a competent garrison in Puebla, this army advanced upon the capital, as follows: Twiggs's division, preceded by Harney's brigade of cavalry, the 7th; Quitman's division of volunteers, with a small detachment of United States' Marines, the 8th; Worth's division, the 9th, and Pillow's division, the 10th—all in this month. On the 8th, I overtook, and then continued with the leading division.

The corps were, at no time, beyond five hours, or supporting distance, apart; and on descending into the basin of the capital (seventy-five miles from Puebla) they became more closely approximated about the head of Lake Chalco, with Lake Tescuco a little in front and to the right.

On the 12th and 13th, we pushed reconnaissances upon the Peñon, an isolated mound (eight miles from Mexico) of great height, strongly fortified to the top (three tiers of works) and flooded around the base by the season of rain and sluices from the lakes. This mound close to the national road, commands the principal approach to the city from the east. No doubt it might have been carried, but at a great and disproportionate loss, and I was anxious to spare the lives of this gallant army for a general battle which I knew we had to win before capturing the city, or obtaining the great object of the campaign—a just and honorable peace.

Another reconnaissance (which I also accompanied) was directed the (13th) upon Mexicalcingo, to the left of the Peñon, a village at a fortified bridge across the outlet or canal, leading from Lake Jochimilco to the capital—five miles from the latter. It might have been easy (masking the Peñon) to force this passage; but on the other side of the bridge, we should have found ourselves four miles from this (San Augustin) road, on a narrow causeway, flanked on the right and left by water or boggy ground.

Those difficulties, closely viewed, threw me back upon the project, long entertained, of turning the strong eastern defences of the city, by passing around south of Lake Chalco and Jochimilco, at the foot of the hills and mountains, so as to reach this point (San Augustin), and hence to manœuvre, on hard ground, though much broken, to the south and southwest of the capital, which has been more or less under our view, since the 10th instant.

Accordingly, by a sudden inversion—Worth's division, with Harney's cavalry brigade, leading—we marched on the 15th instant. Pillow's and Quitman's divisions followed closely, and then Twiggs's division, which was left till the next day at Ayotla, in order to threaten the Peñon and Mexicalcingo, and to deceive the enemy as long as practicable.

Twiggs, on the 16th, marching from Ayotla toward Chalco (six miles), met a corps of more than double his numbers—cavalry and infantry—under General Valencia. Twiggs halted, deployed into line, and by a few rounds from Captain Taylor's field battery, dispersed the enemy, killing or wounding many men and horses. No other molestation has been experienced except a few random shots from guerilleros on the heights; and the march of twenty-seven miles, over a route deemed impracticable by the enemy, is now accomplished by all the corps—thanks to their indomitable zeal and physical energy.

Arriving here, the 18th, Worth's division and Harney's cavalry were pushed forward a league, to reconnoitre and to carry, or to mask, San Antonio on the direct road to the capital. This village was found strongly defended by field works, heavy guns, and a numerous garrison. It could only be turned by infantry, to the left, over a field of volcanic stones and lava; for, to our right, the ground was boggy.

It was soon ascertained by the daring engineers, Captain Mason and Lieutenants Stevens and Tower, that the point could only be approached by the front, over a narrow causeway, flanked with wet ditches of great depth. Worth was ordered not to attack, but to threaten and to mask the place.

The first shot fired from San Antonio (the 18th) killed Captain S. Thornton, 2d Dragoons, a gallant officer, who was covering the operations with his company.

The same day, a reconnaissance was commenced to the left of San Augustin, first over difficult grounds, and farther on, over the same field of volcanic matter which extends to the mountains, some five miles from San Antonio, toward Magdalena. This reconnaissance was continued to-day by Captain Lee, assisted by Lieutenants Beauregard and Tower, all of the Engineers; who were joined in the afternoon by Major Smith of the same corps. Other divisions coming up, Pillow's was advanced to make a practicable road for heavy artillery, and Twiggs's thrown farther in front, to cover that operation; for, by the partial reconnaissance of yesterday, Captain Lee discovered a large corps of observation in that direction, with a detachment of which his supports of cavalry and foot under Captain Kearny and Lieutenant-Colonel Graham, respectively, had a successful skirmish.

By three o'clock this afternoon, the advanced divisions came to a point where the new road could only be continued under the direct fire of twenty-two pieces of the enemy's artillery (most of them of large calibre) placed in a strong intrenched camp to oppose our operations, and surrounded by every advantage of ground, besides immense bodies of cavalry and infantry hourly reënforced from the city, over an excellent road beyond the volcanic field, and consequently beyond the reach of our cavalry and artillery.

Arriving on the ground an hour later, I found that Pillow's and Twiggs's divisions had advanced to dislodge the enemy, picking their way (all officers on foot) along his front, and extending themselves toward the road from the city and the enemy's left. Captain Magruder's field battery, of 12 and 6-pounders, and Lieutenant Callender's battery of mountain howitzers and rockets, had also, with great difficulty, been advanced within range of the intrenched camp. These batteries, most gallantly served, suffered much in the course of the afternoon, from the enemy's superior weight of metal.

The battle, though mostly stationary, continued to rage with great violence until nightfall. Brevet Brigadier-General P. F. Smith's and Brevet Colonel Riley's brigades (Twiggs's division), supported by Brigadier-Generals Pierce's and Cadwallader's brigades (Pillow's division), were more than three hours under a heavy fire of artillery and musketry along the almost impassable ravine in front and to the left of the intrenched camp.

Besides the twenty-two pieces of artillery, the camp and ravine were defended closely by masses of infantry, and these again supported by clouds of cavalry at hand, hovering in view. Consequently no decided impression could be made by daylight on the enemy's most formidable position, because, independently of the difficulty of the ravine, our infantry, unaccompanied by cavalry and artillery, could not advance in column without being mowed down by the grape and canister of the batteries, nor advance in line without being ridden over by the enemy's numerous cavalry. All our corps, however, including Magruder's and Callender's light batteries, not only maintained the exposed positions early gained, but all attempted charges upon them, respectively—particularly on Riley, twice closely engaged with cavalry in greatly superior numbers— were repulsed and punished.

From an eminence, soon after arriving near the

scene, I observed the church and hamlet of Contreras (or Ansalda) on the road leading up from the capital through the intrenched camp to Magdalena, and seeing, at the same time, the stream of reënforcements advancing by that road from the city, I ordered (through Major-General Pillow) Colonel Morgan with his regiment, the 15th, till then held in reserve by Pillow, to move forward and to occupy Contreras (or Ansalda)—being persuaded, if occupied, it would arrest the enemy's reënforcements and ultimately decide the battle.

Riley was already on the enemy's left, in advance of the hamlet. A few minutes later, Brigadier-General Shields with his volunteer brigade (New York and South Carolina regiments—Quitman's division) coming up under my orders from San Augustin, I directed Shields to follow and sustain Morgan. These corps, over the extreme difficulties of ground—partially covered with a low forest—before described, reached Contreras, and found Cadwallader's brigade in position, observing the formidable movement from the capital, and much needing the timely reënforcement.

It was already dark, and the cold rain had begun to fall in torrents upon our unsheltered troops ; for the hamlet, though a strong defensive position, could only hold the wounded men, and, unfortunately, the new regiments have little or nothing to eat in their haver-sacks. Wet, hungry, and without the possibility of sleep; all our gallant corps, I learn, are full of confidence, and only wait for the last hour of darkness to gain the positions whence to storm and carry the enemy's works.

Of the seven officers despatched since about sun-down, from my position opposite to the enemy's centre, and on this side of the volcanic field—to communicate instructions to the hamlet—not one has succeeded in getting through these difficulties increased by darkness. They have all returned. But the gallant and inde-fatigable Captain Lee, of the Engineers, who has been constantly with the operating forces, is (eleven o'clock P. M.,) just in from Shields, Smith, Cadwallader, etc., to report as above, and to ask that a powerful diversion be made against the centre of the intrenched camp toward morning.

Brigadier-General Twiggs cut off as above, from the part of his division beyond the impracticable ground, and Captain Lee are gone, under my orders, to collect the forces remaining on this side with which to make that diversion at about five o'clock in the morning.

And here I will end this report, commenced at its date, and in another, continue the narrative of the great events which now impend.

I have the honor to be, etc., etc.,

WINFIELD SCOTT.

Hon. Wm. L. Marcy, *Secretary of War.*

CHAPTER XXXI.

Report No. 32.

HEADQUARTERS OF THE ARMY,
TACUBAYA, AT THE GATES OF
MEXICO, *August* 28, 1847.

SIR:

My report, No. 31, commenced in the night of the 19th instant, closed with the operations of the army on that day.

The morning of the 20th opened with one of a series of unsurpassed achievements, all in view of the capital, and to which I shall give the general name—*Battles of Mexico.*

In the night of the 19th, Brigadier-Generals Shields,

P. F. Smith, and Cadwallader, and Colonel Riley, with their brigades, and the 15th Regiment, under Colonel Morgan, detached from Brigadier - General Pierce—found themselves in and about the important position —the village, hamlet or *hacienda*, called indifferently, Contreras, Ansalda, San Geronimo—half a mile nearer to the city than the enemy's intrenched camp, on the same road, toward the factory of Magdalena.

That camp had been, unexpectedly, our formidable point of attack in the afternoon before, and we had now to take it, without the aid of cavalry or artillery, or to throw back our advanced corps upon the direct road from San Augustin to the city, and thence force a passage through San Antonio.

Accordingly, to meet contingencies, Major-General Worth was ordered to leave early in the morning of the 20th, one of his brigades to mask San Antonio, and to march with the other six miles, *via* San Augustin, upon Contreras. A like destination was given to Major-General Quitman and his remaining brigade in San Augustin—replacing, for the moment, the garrison of that important dépôt with Harney's brigade of cavalry, as horse could not pass over the intervening lava, etc., to reach the field of battle.

A diversion for an earlier hour (daylight) had been arranged the night before, according to the suggestion of Brigadier-General P. F. Smith, received through the Engineer, Captain Lee, who conveyed my orders to our troops remaining on the ground, opposite to the enemy's centre—the point for the diversion or a real attack, as circumstances might allow.

Guided by Captain Lee, it proved the latter, under the command of Colonel Ransom of the 9th, having with him that regiment and some companies of three others—the 3d, 12th, and Rifles.

Shields, the senior officer at the hamlet, having arrived in the night, after Smith had arranged with Cadwallader and Riley the plan of attack for the morning, delicately waived interference; but reserved to himself the double task of holding the hamlet with his two regiments (South Carolina and New York Volunteers) against ten times his numbers on the side of the city, including the slopes to his left, and in case the enemy's camp in his rear should be carried, to face about and cut off the flying enemy.

At three o'clock A. M. the great movement commenced on the rear of the enemy's camp, Riley leading, followed successively by Cadwallader's and Smith's brigades, the latter temporarily under the orders of Major Dimick of the 1st Artillery—the whole force being commanded by Smith, the senior in the general attack, and whose arrangements, skill, and gallantry always challenge the highest admiration.

The march was rendered tedious by the darkness, rain, and mud; but about sunrise, Riley, conducted by Lieutenant Tower, Engineer, had reached an elevation behind the enemy, whence he precipitated his columns; stormed the intrenchments, planted his several colors upon them, and carried the work—all in seventeen minutes.

Conducted by Lieutenant Beauregard, Engineer, and Lieutenant Brooks of Twiggs's Staff—both of whom, like Lieutenant Tower, had, in the night, twice reconnoitred the ground—Cadwallader brought up to the general assault, two of his regiments—the Voltigeurs and the 11th; and at the appointed time Colonel Ransom, with his temporary brigade, conducted by Captain Lee, Engineer, not only made the movement in front, to divert and to distract the enemy, but, after crossing the deep ravine, advanced, and poured into the works and upon the fugitives many volleys from his destructive musketry.

In tho mean time Smith's own brigade, under the temporary command of Major Dimick, following the movements of Riley and Cadwallader, discovered, opposite to, and outside of the works, a long line of Mexican cavalry, drawn up as a support. Dimick having at the head of the brigade the company of Sappers and Miners, under Lieutenant G. W. Smith, Engineer, who had conducted the march, was ordered by Brigadier-General Smith to form his line faced to the enemy, and in a charge, against a flank, routed the cavalry.

Shields, too, by the wise disposition of his brigade and gallant activity, contributed much to the general results. He held masses of cavalry and infantry, supported by artillery, in check below him, and captured hundreds, with one general (Mendoza), of those who fled from above.

I doubt whether a more brilliant or decisive victory —taking into view ground, artificial defences, batteries, and the extreme disparity of numbers—without cavalry or artillery on our side—is to be found on record. Including all our corps directed against the intrenched camp, with Shields's brigade at the hamlet, we positively did not number over four thousand five hundred rank and file; and we knew by sight, and since, more

21

certainly, by many captured documents and letters, that the enemy had actually engaged on the spot seven thousand men, with at least twelve thousand more hovering within sight and striking distance—both on the 19th and 20th. All, not killed or captured, now fled with precipitation.

Thus was the great victory of Contreras achieved; one road to the capital opened; seven hundred of the enemy killed; eight hundred and thirteen prisoners, including, among eighty-eight officers, four generals; besides many colors and standards; twenty-two pieces of brass ordnance—half of large calibre; thousands of small arms and accoutrements; an immense quantity of shot, shells, powder, and cartridges; seven hundred pack mules, many horses, etc., etc.—all in our hands.

It is highly gratifying to find that, by skilful arrangement and rapidity of execution, our loss, in killed and wounded, did not exceed, on the spot, sixty— among the former the brave Captain Charles Hanson, of the 4th Infantry—not more distinguished for gallantry than for modesty, morals, and piety. Lieutenant J. P. Johnstone, 1st Artillery, serving with Magruder's battery, a young officer of the highest promise, was killed the evening before.

One of the most pleasing incidents of the victory is the recapture, in their works, by Captain Drum, 4th Artillery, under Major Gardner, of the two brass 6-pounders, taken from another company of the same regiment, though without the loss of honor, at the glorious battle of Buena Vista—about which guns the whole regiment had mourned for so many long months! Coming up a little later I had the happiness to join in the protracted cheers of the gallant 4th on the joyous event; and, indeed, the whole army sympathizes in its just pride and exultation.

The battle being won before the advancing brigades of Worth's and Quitman's divisions were in sight, both were ordered back to their late positions:—Worth, to attack San Antonio, in front, with his whole force, as soon as approached in the rear by Pillow's and Twiggs's divisions—moving from Contreras, through San Angel and Coyoacan. By carrying San Antonio, we knew that we should open another—a shorter and better road to the capital for our siege and other trains.

Accordingly, the two advanced divisions and Shields brigade marched from Contreras, under the immediate orders of Major-General Pillow, who was now joined by the gallant Brigadier-General Pierce of his division, personally thrown out of activity, late the evening before, by a severe hurt received from the fall of his horse.   .

After giving necessary orders on the field, in the midst of prisoners and trophies, and sending instructions to Harney's brigade of cavalry (left at San Augustin) to join me, I personally followed Pillow's command.

Arriving at Coyoacan, two miles by a cross road, from the rear of San Antonio, I first detached Captain Lee, Engineer, with Captain Kearny's troop, 1st Dragoons, supported by the Rifle Regiment, under Major Loring, to reconnoitre that strong point; and next despatched Major-General Pillow, with one of his brigades (Cadwallader's), to make the attack upon it, in concert with Major-General Worth on the opposite side.

At the same time, by another road to the left, Lieutenant Stevens of the Engineers, supported by Lieutenant G. W. Smith's company of sappers and miners, of the same corps, was sent to reconnoitre the strongly fortified church or convent of San Pablo, in the hamlet of Churubusco—one mile off. Twiggs with one of his brigades (Smith's—less the Rifles) and Captain Taylor's field battery, were ordered to follow and to attack the convent. Major Smith, senior Engineer, was despatched to concert with Twiggs the mode and means of attack, and Twiggs's other brigade (Riley's) I soon ordered up to support him.

Next (but all in ten minutes) I sent Pierce (just able to keep the saddle) with his brigade (Pillow's division), conducted by Captain Lee, Engineer, by a third road a little farther to our left, to attack the enemy's right and rear, in order to favor the movement upon the convent, and to cut off a retreat toward the capital. And finally, Shields, senior brigadier to Pierce, with the New York and South Carolina Volunteers (Quitman's division), was ordered to follow Pierce closely, and to take the command of our left wing All these movements were made with the utmost alacrity by our gallant troops and commanders.

Finding myself at Coyoacan, from which so many roads conveniently branched, without escort or reserve, I had to advance for safety close upon Twiggs's rear. The battle now raged from the right to the left of our whole line.

Learning on the return of Captain Lee, that Shields in the rear of Churubusco was hard pressed, and in danger of being outflanked, if not overwhelmed, by greatly superior numbers, I immediately sent under Major Sumner, 2d Dragoons, the Rifles (Twiggs's reserve) and Captain Sibley's troop, 2d Dragoons, then at hand, to support our left, guided by the same engineer.

About an hour earlier, Worth had, by skilful and daring movements upon the front and right, turned and forced San Antonio—its garrison, no doubt, much shaken by our decisive victory at Contreras.

His second brigade (Colonel Clarke's) conducted by Captain Mason, Engineer, assisted by Lieutenant Hardcastle, Topographical Engineer, turned to the left, and by a wide sweep came out upon the high road to the capital. At this point the heavy garrison (three thousand men) in retreat was, by Clarke, cut in the centre : one portion, the rear, driven upon Dolores, off to the right, and the other upon Churubusco, in the direct line of our operations. The first brigade (Colonel Garland's), same division, consisting of the 2d Artillery, under Major Galt, the 3d Artillery, under Lieutenant-Colonel Belton, and the 4th Infantry, commanded by Major F. Lee, with Lieutenant-Colonel Duncan's field battery (temporarily) followed in pursuit through the town, taking one general prisoner, the abandoned guns (five pieces), much ammunition, and other public property.

The forcing of San Antonio was the *second* brilliant event of the day.

Worth's division being soon reunited in hot pursuit, he was joined by Major-General Pillow, who, marching from Coyoacan and discovering that San Antonio had been carried, immediately turned to the left according to my instructions, and, though much impeded by ditches and swamps, hastened to the attack of Churubusco.

The hamlet or scattered houses bearing this name, presented besides the fortified convent, a strong field-work (*tête de pont*) with regular bastions and curtains at the head of a bridge over which the road passes from San Antonio to the capital.

The whole remaining forces of Mexico—some twenty-seven thousand men—cavalry, artillery, and infantry, collected from every quarter—were now in, on the flanks, or within supporting distance of those works, and seemed resolved to make a last and desperate stand ; for if beaten here, the feebler defences at the gates of the city—four miles off—could not, as was well known to both parties, delay the victors an hour.   [?]

The capital of an ancient empire, now of a great republic; or an early peace, the assailants were resolved to win. Not an American—and we were less than a third of the enemy's numbers—had a doubt as to the result.

The fortified church or convent, hotly pressed by Twiggs, had already held out about an hour, when Worth and Pillow—the latter having with him Cadwallader's brigade—began to manœuvre closely upon the *tête de pont*, with the convent at half gunshot to their left. Garland's brigade (Worth's division), to which had been added the light battalion under Lieutenant-Colonel C. F. Smith, continued to advance in front and under the fire of a long line of infantry off on the left of the bridge; and Clarke of the same division, directed his brigade along the road or close by its side. Two of Pillow's and Cadwallader's regiments, the 11th and 14th, supported and participated in this direct movement: the other (the voltigeurs) was left in reserve. Most of these corps—particularly Clarke's brigade—advancing perpendicularly, were made to suffer much by the fire of the *tête de pont*, and they would have suffered greatly more by flank attacks from the convent, but for the pressure of Twiggs on the other side of that work.

This well-combined and daring movement at length reached the principal point of attack, and the formidable *tête de pont* was at once assaulted and carried by the bayonet. Its deep wet ditch was first gallantly crossed by the 8th and 5th Infantry, commanded respectively by Major Waite and Lieutenant-Colonel Martin Scott—followed closely by the 6th Infantry (same brigade), which had been so much exposed on the road—the 11th regiment, under Lieutenant-Colonel Graham, and the 14th commanded by Colonel Trousdale, both of Cadwallader's brigade, Pillow's division. About the same time, the enemy in front of Garland, after a hot conflict of an hour and a half gave way, in a retreat toward the capital.

The immediate results of this *third* signal triumph of the day were three field pieces, one hundred and ninety-two prisoners, much ammunition and two colors taken at the *tête de pont.*

Lieutenant I. F. Irons, 1st Artillery, aide-de-camp to Brigadier-General Cadwallader, a young officer of great merit and conspicuous in battle on several previous occasions, received in front of the work, a mortal wound. (Since dead.)

As the concurrent attack upon the convent favored,

21*

physically and morally, the assault upon the *tête de pont*, so reciprocally, no doubt, the fall of the latter contributed to the capture of the former. The two works were only some four hundred and fifty yards apart; and as soon as we were in possession of the *tête de pont*, a captured 4-pounder was turned and fired—first by Captain Larkin Smith, and next by Lieutenant Snelling, both of the 8th Infantry—several times upon the convent. In the same brief interval, Lieutenant-Colonel Duncan (also of Worth's division) gallantly brought two of his guns to bear at a short range from the San Antonio road, upon the principal face of the work and on the tower of the church, which in the obstinate contest, had been often refilled with some of the best sharpshooters of the enemy.

Finally, twenty minutes after the *tête de pont* had been carried by Worth and Pillow, and at the end of a desperate conflict of two hours and a half, the church or convent—the citadel of the strong line of defence along the rivulet of Churubusco—yielded to Twiggs's division, and threw out on all sides signals of surrender. The white flags, however, were not exhibited until the moment when the 3d infantry, under Captain Alexander, had cleared the way by fire and bayonet, and had entered the work. Captain I. M. Smith and Lieutenant O. L. Shepherd, both of that regiment, with their companies, had the glory of leading the assault. The former received the surrender, and Captain Alexander instantly hung out from the balcony the colors of the gallant 3d. Major Dimick with a part of the 1st Artillery, serving as infantry, entered nearly abreast with the leading troops.

Captain Taylor's field battery, attached to Twiggs's division, opened its effective fire at an early moment upon the outworks of the convent and the tower of its church. Exposed to the severest fire of the enemy, the captain, his officers and men, won universal admiration; but at length much disabled in men and horses, the battery was by superior orders withdrawn from the action, thirty minutes before the surrender of the convent.

Those corps, excepting Taylor's battery, belonged to the brigade of Brigadier-General P. F. Smith, who closely directed the whole attack in front with his habitual coolness and ability; while Riley's brigade— the 2d and 7th Infantry, under Captain T. Morris and Lieutenent-Colonel Plympton respectively—vigorously engaged the right of the work and part of its rear.

At the moment the Rifles, belonging to Smith's, were detached in support of Brigadier-General Shields's on our extreme left, and the 4th Artillery, acting as infantry, under Major Gardner, belonging to Riley's brigade, had been left in charge of the camp, trophies, etc., at Contreras. Twiggs's division at Churubusco had thus been deprived of the services of two of its most gallant and effective regiments.

The immediate results of this victory were :—the capture of seven field pieces, some ammunition, one color, three generals, and one thousand two hundred and sixty-one prisoners, including other officers.

Captains E. A. Capron and M. I. Burke, and Lieutenant S. Hoffman, all of the 1st Artillery, and Captain J. W. Anderson and Lieutenant Thomas Easley, both of the 2d Infantry—five officers of great merit—fell gallantly before this work.

The capture of the enemy's citadel was the *fourth* great achievement of our arms in the same day.

It has been stated that some two hours and a half before, Pierce's, followed closely by the volunteer brigade —both under the command of Brigadier-General Shields —had been despatched to our left to turn the enemy's works ;—to prevent the escape of the garrisons and to oppose the extension of the enemy's numerous corps from the rear upon and around our left.

Considering the inferior numbers of the two brigades, the objects of the movement were difficult to accomplish. Hence the reënforcement (the Rifles, etc.) sent forward a little later.

In a winding march of a mile around to the right, this temporary division found itself on the edge of an open wet meadow, near the road from San Antonio to the capital, and in the presence of some four thousand of the enemy's infantry, a little in rear of Churubusco, on that road. Establishing the right at a strong building, Shields extended his left parallel to the road, to outflank the enemy toward the capital. But the enemy extending his right supported by three thousand cavalry more rapidly (being favored by better ground), in the same direction, Shields concentrated the division about a hamlet and determined to attack in front. The battle was long, hot and varied; but ultimately, success crowned the zeal and gallantry of our troops, ably directed by their distinguished commander, Brigadier-General Shields. The 9th, 12th, and 15th Regiments, under Colonel Ransom, Captain Wood, and Colonel Morgan respectively, of Pierce's brigade (Pillow's division), and the New York and South Carolina Volunteers, under Colonels Burnett and Butler, respectively, of Shields's own brigade (Quitman's division), together with the mountain howitzer battery, now under Lieutenant Reno of the Ordnance Corps, all shared in the glory of this action—our *fifth* victory in the same day.

Brigadier-General Pierce, from the hurt of the evening before—under pain and exhaustion—fainted in the action. Several other changes in command occurred on this field. Thus Colonel Morgan being severely wounded, the command of the 15th Infantry devolved on Lieutenant-Colonel Howard; Colonel Burnett receiving a like wonnd, the command of the New York Volunteers fell to Lieutenant-Colonel Baxter; and, on the fall of the lamented Colonel P. M. Butler—earlier badly wounded, but continuing to lead nobly in the hottest part of the battle—the command of the South Carolina Volunteers devolved—first, on Lieutenant-Colonel Dickinson, who being severely wounded (as before in the siege of Vera Cruz), the regiment ultimately fell under the orders of Major Gladden.

Lieutenants David Adams and W. R. Williams of the same corps; Captain Augustus Quarles and Lieutenant J. B. Goodman of the 15th, and Lieutenant E. Chandler, New York Volunteers—all gallant officers, nobly fell in the same action.

Shields took three hundred and eighty prisoners, including officers ; and it cannot be doubted that the rage of the conflict between him and the enemy, just in the rear of the *tête de pont* and the convent, had some influence on the surrender of those formidable defences.

As soon as the *tête de pont* was carried, the greater part of Worth's and Pillow's forces passed that bridge in rapid pursuit of the flying enemy. These distinguished generals, coming up with Brigadier-General Shields, now also victorious, the three continued to press upon the fugitives to within a mile and a half of the capital. Here, Colonel Harney, with a small part of his brigade of cavalry, rapidly passed to the front, and charged the enemy up to the nearest gate.

The cavalry charge was headed by Captain Kearny, of the 1st Dragoons, having in squadron with his own troop, that of Captain McReynolds of the 3d—making the usual escort to general headquarters ; but, being early in the day detached for general service, was now under Colonel Harney's orders. The gallant captain not hearing the *recall*, that had been sounded, dashed up to the San Antonio gate, sabring in his way all who resisted. Of the seven officers of the squadron, Kearny lost his left arm; McReynolds and Lieutenant Lorimer Graham were both severely wounded, and Lieutenant R. S. Ewell, who succeeded to the command of the escort, had two horses killed under him. Major F. D. Mills, of the 15th infantry, a volunteer in this charge, was killed at the gate.

So terminated the series of events which I have but feebly presented. My thanks were freely poured out on the different fields—to the abilities and science of generals and other officers—to the zeal and prowess of all—the rank and file included. But a reward infinitely higher—the applause of a grateful country and Government—will, I cannot doubt, be accorded, in due time, to so much merit of every sort, displayed by this glorious army, which has now overcome all difficulties —distance, climate, ground, fortifications, numbers.

It has in a single day, in many battles, as often defeated thirty-two thousand men; made about three thousand prisoners, including eight generals (two of them ex-presidents) and two hundred and five other officers; killed or wounded four thousand of all ranks

—besides entire corps dispersed and dissolved; captured thirty-seven pieces of ordnance—more than trebling our siege train and field batteries—with a large number of small arms, a full supply of ammunition of every kind, etc., etc.

These great results have overwhelmed the enemy. Our loss amounts to one thousand and fifty-three— *killed*, one hundred and thirty-nine, including sixteen officers; *wounded*, eight hundred and seventy-six, with sixty officers. The greater number of the dead and disabled were of the highest worth. Those under treatment, thanks to our very able medical officers, are generally doing well.

I regret having been obliged, on the 20th, to leave Major-General Quitman, an able commander, with a part of his division—the fine 2d Pennsylvania Volunteers, and the veteran detachment of United States' Marines—at our important dépôt, San Augustin. It was there that I had placed our sick and wounded; the siege, supply, and baggage trains. If these had been lost, the army would have been driven almost to despair; and considering the enemy's very great excess of numbers, and the many approaches to the dépôt, it might well have become, emphatically, *the post of honor*.

After so many victories, we might, with but little additional loss, have occupied the capital the same evening. [?]   But Mr. Trist, commissioner, etc., as well as myself, had been admonished by the best friends of peace—intelligent neutrals and some American residents—against precipitation ; lest, by wantonly driving away the government and others—dishonored—we might scatter the elements of peace, excite a spirit of national desperation, and thus indefinitely postpone the hope of accommodation.*

Deeply impressed with this danger, and remembering our mission—*to conquer a peace*—the army very cheerfully sacrificed to patriotism—to the great wish and want of our country—the *éclat* that would have followed an entrance—sword in hand—into a great

---

* There were other reasons such as are alluded to in my report of the capture of Vera Cruz. If we had proceeded to assault the city by daylight our loss would have been dangerously great, and if a little later in the night, the slain, on the other side, including men, women, and children, would have been frightful, because if the assailants stopped to make prisoners before occupying all the strongholds, they would soon become prisoners themselves. Other atrocities, by the victors, are, in such cases, inevitable. Pillage always follows, and seems authorized by the usage of war. Hence I promised (September 13), at the gates of Mexico, a contribution in lieu of pillage, in order to avoid the horrors in question, and the consequent loss of discipline and efficiency.

capital. Willing to leave something to this republic—of no immediate value to us—on which to rest her pride, and to recover temper—I halted our victorious corps at the gates of the city (at least for a time), and have them now cantoned in the neighboring villages, where they are well sheltered and supplied with all necessaries.

On the morning of the 21st, being about to take up battering or assaulting positions, to authorize me to summon the city to surrender, or to sign an armistice with a pledge to enter at once into negotiations for peace—a mission came out to propose a truce. Rejecting its terms, I despatched my contemplated note to President Santa Anna—omitting the summons. The 22d, commissioners were appointed by the commanders of the two armies; the armistice was signed the 23d, and ratifications exchanged the 24th.

All matters in dispute between the two governments have been thus happily turned over to their plenipotentiaries, who have now had several conferences, and with, I think, some hope of signing a treaty of peace.

There will be transmitted to the Adjutant-General reports from divisions, brigades, etc., on the foregoing operations, to which I must refer, with my hearty concurrence in the just applause bestowed on corps and individuals by their respective commanders. I have been able—this report being necessarily a summary—to bring out, comparatively, but little of individual merit not lying directly in the way of the narrative. Thus I doubt whether I have, in express terms, given my approbation and applause to the commanders of divisions and independent brigades; but left their fame upon higher grounds—the simple record of their great deeds and the brilliant results.*

To the staff, both general and personal, attached to general headquarters, I was again under high obligations for services in the field, as always in the bureaux. I add their names, etc.: Lieutenant-Colonel Hitchcock, Acting Inspector-General; Major J. L. Smith, Captain R. E. Lee (as distinguished for felicitous execution as

---

* *Litera scripta manet.* In this edition of my reports of battles, etc., I, of course, expunge none of the praises therein bestowed on certain division and brigade commanders; but as a caution to future generals-in-chief I must say I soon had abundant reason to know, that I had in haste too confidently relied upon the partial statements of several of those commanders respecting their individual skill and prowess, and the merits of a few of their favorites—subordinates. I except from this remark, Generals Quitman, Shields, P. F. Smith, N. S. Clarke, Riley, and Cadwallader.

for science and daring), Captain Mason, Lieutenants Stevens, Beauregard, Tower, G. W. Smith, George B. McClellan, and Foster—all of the Engineers; Major Turnbull, Captain J. McClellan, and Lieutenant Hardcastle, Topographical Engineers; Captain Huger and Lieutenant Hagner, of the Ordnance; Captains Irwin and Wayne, of the Quartermaster's Department; Captain Grayson, of the Commissariat; Surgeon-General Lawson, in his particular department; Captain H. L. Scott, Acting Adjutant-General; Lieutenant T. Williams, Aide-de-Camp, and Lieutenant Lay, Military Secretary.

Lieutenant Schuyler Hamilton,* another aide-de-camp, had a week before been thrown out of activity by a severe wound received in a successful charge of

---

* This gallant, intelligent officer being sent with a detachment of cavalry from Chalco to an iron foundery, some fifteen miles off, beyond Mira Flores, to make contingent arrangements for shots and shells—we having brought up but few of either, from the want of road power—returning, fell into an ambuscade, and though he cut his way through, was, while slaying one man in his front, pierced through the body with a lance, by another, and thus thrown *hors de combat* for the remainder of the campaign. In 1861, he, as a private, was in one of the first regiments of volunteers that hastened to the defence of Washington;—again became one of my aides-de-camp, and, in succession, a distinguished brigadier and major-general of volunteers in the Southwest.

cavalry against cavalry, and four times his numbers; but on the 20th, I had the valuable services, as volunteer aids, of Majors Kirby and Van Buren, of the Pay Department, always eager for activity and distinction, and of a third, the gallant Major J. P. Gaines, of the Kentucky Volunteers.

I have the honor to be, etc., etc.,

WINFIELD SCOTT.

Hon. Wm. L. Marcy, *Secretary of War.*

CHAPTER XXXII.

Report No. 33.

HEADQUARTERS OF THE ARMY,
TACUBAYA, NEAR MEXICO,
September 11, 1847.

SIR:

I have heretofore reported that I had, August 24, concluded an armistice with President Santa Anna, which was promptly followed by meetings between Mr. Trist and Mexican commissioners appointed to treat of peace.

Negotiations were actively continued with, as was

understood, some prospect of a successful result up to the 2d instant, when our commissioner handed in his *ultimatum* (on boundaries), and the negotiators adjourned to meet again on the 6th.

Some infractions of the truce in respect to our supplies from the city, were earlier committed, followed by apologies on the part of the enemy. These vexations I was willing to put down to the imbecility of the government, and waived any pointed demands of reparation while any hope remained of a satisfactory termination of the war. But on the 5th, and more fully on the 6th, I learned that as soon as the *ultimatum* had been considered in a grand council of ministers and others, President Santa Anna on the 4th or 5th, without giving me the slightest notice, actively recommenced strengthening the military defences of the city, in gross violation of the 3d article of the armistice.

On that information, which has since received the fullest verification, I addressed to him my note of the 6th. His reply, dated the same day, received the next morning, was absolutely and notoriously false, both in recrimination and explanation. I enclose copies of both papers, and have had no subsequent correspondence with the enemy.

Being delayed by the terms of the armistice more than two weeks, we had now, late on the 7th, to begin to reconnoitre the different approaches to the city, within our reach, before I could lay down any definitive plan of attack.

The same afternoon a large body of the enemy was discovered hovering about the *Molinos del Rey*, within a mile and a third of this village, where I am quartered with the general staff and Worth's division.

It might have been supposed that an attack upon us was intended; but knowing the great value to the enemy of those mills (*Molinos del Rey*), containing a cannon foundery, with a large deposite of powder in *Casa Mata* near them; and having heard two days before that many church bells had been sent out to be cast into guns, the enemy's movement was easily understood, and I resolved at once to drive him early the next morning, to seize the powder, and to destroy the foundery.

Another motive for this decision—leaving the general plan of attack upon the city for full reconnaissance—was, that we knew our recent captures had left the enemy not a fourth of the guns necessary to arm, all at the same time, the strong works at each of the eight

22

city gates; and we could not cut the communication between the foundery and the capital without first taking the formidable castle on the heights of Chapultepec, which overlooked both and stood between.

For this difficult operation we were not entirely ready, and moreover we might altogether neglect the castle, if, as we then hoped, our reconnaissances should prove that the distant southern approaches to the city were more eligible than this southwestern one.

Hence the decision promptly taken, the execution of which was assigned to Brevet Major-General Worth, whose division was reënforced with Cadwallader's brigade of Pillow's division, three squadrons of dragoons under Major Sumner, and some heavy guns of the siege train under Captain Huger of the Ordnance, and Captain Drum of the 4th Artillery—two officers of the highest merit.

For the decisive and brilliant results, I beg to refer to the report of the immediate commander, Major-General Worth, in whose commendations of the gallant officers and men—dead and living—I heartily concur; having witnessed, but with little interference, their noble devotion to fame and to country.

The enemy having several times reënforced his line,

and the action soon becoming much more general than I had expected, I called up, from the distance of three miles, first Major-General Pillow, with his remaining brigade (Pierce's); and next Riley's brigade of Twiggs's division—leaving his other brigade (Smith's) in observation at San Angel. Those corps approached with zeal and rapidity; but the battle was won just as Brigadier-General Pierce reached the ground, and had interposed his corps between Garland's brigade (Worth's division) and the retreating enemy.

The accompanying report mentions, with just commendation, two of my volunteer aids—Major Kirby, Paymaster, and Major Gaines, of the Kentucky Volunteers. I also had the valuable services, on the same field, of several other officers of my staff, general and personal: Lieutenant-Colonel Hitchcock, Acting Inspector-General; Captain R. E. Lee, Engineer; Captain Irwin, Chief Quartermaster; Captain Grayson, Chief Commissary; Captain H. L. Scott, Acting Adjutant-General; Lieutenant Williams, Aide-de-Camp; and Lieutenant Lay, Military Secretary.

I have the honor to be, etc., etc.,

WINFIELD SCOTT.

Hon. Wm. L. Marcy, *Secretary of War.*

Report No. 34.

HEADQUARTERS OF THE ARMY,
NATIONAL PALACE OF MEXICO,
September 18, 1847.

SIR :

At the end of another series of arduous and brilliant operations, of more than forty-eight hours' continuance, this glorious army hoisted, on the morning of the 14th, the colors of the United States on the walls of this palace.

The victory of the 8th, at the Molinos del Rey, was followed by daring reconnaissances on the part of our distinguished engineers—Captain Lee, Lieutenants Beauregard, Stevens and Tower—Major Smith, senior, being sick, and Captain Mason, third in rank, wounded. Their operations were directed principally to the south—toward the gates of the Piedad, San Angel, (Niño Perdido), San Antonio, and the Paseo de la Viga.

This city stands on a slight swell of ground, near the centre of an irregular basin, and is girdled with a ditch in its greater extent—a navigable canal of great breadth and depth—very difficult to bridge in the presence of an enemy, and serving at once for drainage, custom-house purposes, and military defence; leaving eight entrances or gates, over arches—each of which we found defended by a system of strong works, that seemed to require nothing but some men and guns to be impregnable.

Outside and within the cross-fires of those gates, we found to the south other obstacles but little less formidable. All the approaches near the city are over elevated causeways, cut in many places (to oppose us), and flanked on both sides by ditches, also of unusual dimensions. The numerous cross-roads are flanked in like manner, having bridges at the intersections, recently broken. The meadows thus checkered, are, moreover, in many spots, under water or marshy; for, it will be remembered, we were in the midst of the wet season, though with less rain than usual, and we could not wait for the fall of the neighboring lakes and the consequent drainage of the wet grounds at the edge of the city—the lowest in the whole basin.

After a close personal survey of the southern gates, covered by Pillow's division and Riley's brigade of Twiggs's—with four times our numbers concentrated in our immediate front—I determined, on the 11th, to avoid that network of obstacle, and to seek, by a sudden inversion to the southwest and west, less unfavorable approaches.

To economize the lives of our gallant officers and men, as well as to insure success, it became indispensable that this resolution should be long masked from the enemy; and again, that the new movement when discovered, should be mistaken for a feint, and the old as indicating our true and ultimate point of attack.

Accordingly, on the spot, the 11th, I ordered Quitman's division from Coyoacan, to join Pillow *by daylight* before the southern gates, and then that the two major-generals with their divisions, should *by night* proceed (two miles) to join me at Tacubaya, where I was quartered with Worth's division. Twiggs, with Riley's brigade and Captains Taylor's and Steptoe's field batteries—the latter of 12-pounders—was left in front of those gates to manœuvre, to threaten, or to make false attacks, in order to occupy and deceive the enemy. Twiggs's other brigade (Smith's) was left at supporting distance in the rear at San Angel, till the morning of the 13th, and also to support our general dépôt at Mixcoac. The stratagem against the south was admirably executed throughout the 12th and down to the afternoon of the 13th, when it was too late for the enemy to recover from the effects of his delusion.

The first step in the new movement was to carry Chapultepec, a natural and isolated mound of great elevation, strongly fortified at its base, on its acclivities and heights. Besides a numerous garrison, here was the military college of the republic, with a large number of sub-lieutenants and other students. Those works were within direct gunshot of the village of Tacubaya, and, until carried, we could not approach the city on the west without making a circuit too wide and too hazardous.

In the course of the same night (that of the 11th), heavy batteries within easy ranges were established. No. 1, on our right, under the command of Captain Drum, 4th Artillery (relieved the next day for some hours by Lieutenant Andrews of the 3d), and No. 2, commanded by Lieutenant Hagner, Ordnance—both supported by Quitman's division. Nos. 3 and 4, on the opposite side, supported by Pillow's division, were commanded, the former by Captain Brooks and Lieutenant S. S. Anderson, 2d Artillery, alternately, and the latter by Lieutenant Stone, Ordnance. The batteries were traced by Captain Huger, Ordnance, and

Captain Lee, Engineer, and constructed by them with the able assistance of the young officers of those corps and of the artillery.

To prepare for an assault, it was foreseen that the play of the batteries might run into the second day; but recent captures had not only trebled our siege pieces, but also our ammunition; and we knew that we should greatly augment both by carrying the place. I was, therefore, in no haste in ordering an assault before the works were well crippled by our missiles.

The bombardment and cannonade, under the direction of Captain Huger, were commenced early in the morning of the 12th. Before nightfall, which necessarily stopped our batteries, we had perceived that a good impression had been made on the castle and its outworks, and that a large body of the enemy had remained outside, toward the city, from an early hour, to avoid our fire, but to be at hand on its cessation in order to reënforce the garrison against an assault. The same outside force was discovered the next morning after our batteries had reopened upon the castle, by which we again reduced its garrison to the *minimum* needed for the guns.

Pillow and Quitman had been in position since

early in the night of the 11th. Major-General Worth was now ordered to hold his division in reserve, near the foundery, to support Pillow ; and Brigadier-General Smith, of Twiggs's division, had just arrived with his• brigade from Piedad (two miles), to support Quitman. Twiggs's guns before the southern gates, again reminded us, as the day before, that he, with Riley's brigade and Taylor's and Steptoe's batteries, was in activity threatening the southern gates, and thus holding a great part of the Mexican army on the defensive.

Worth's division furnished Pillow's attack with an assaulting party of some two hundred and fifty volunteer officers and men, under Captain McKenzie, of the 2d Artillery ; and Twiggs's division supplied a similar one, commanded by Captain Casey, 2d Infantry, to Quitman. Each of these little columns was furnished with scaling ladders.

The signal I had appointed for the attack was the momentary cessation of fire on the part of our heavy batteries. About eight o'clock in the morning of the 13th, judging that the time had arrived, by the effect of the missiles we had thrown, I sent an aide-de-camp to Pillow, and another to Quitman, with notice that the concerted signal was about to be given. Both

22*

columns now advanced with an alacrity that gave assurance of prompt success. The batteries, seizing opportunities, threw shots and shells upon the enemy over the heads of our men with good effect, particularly at every attempt to reënforce the works from without to meet our assault.

Major-General Pillow's approach on the west side, lay through an open grove filled with sharpshooters, who were speedily dislodged : when, being up with the front of the attack, and emerging into open space at the foot of a rocky acclivity, that gallant leader was struck down by an agonizing wound. The immediate command devolved on Brigadier-General Cadwallader, in the absence of the senior brigadier (Pierce) of the same division—an invalid since the events of August 19. On a previous call of Pillow, Worth had just sent him a reënforcement—Colonel Clarke's brigade.

The broken acclivity was still to be ascended, and a strong redoubt, midway, to be carried, before reaching the castle on the heights. The advance of our brave men, led by brave officers, though necessarily slow, was unwavering, over rocks, chasms, and mines, and under the hottest fire of cannon and 'musketry. The redoubt now yielded to resistless valor, and the shouts that followed announced to the castle the fate that impended. The enemy were steadily driven from shelter to shelter. The retreat allowed not time to fire a single mine, without the certainty of blowing up friend and foe. Those who, at a distance, attempted to apply matches to the long trains, were shot down by our men. There was death below, as well as above ground. At length the ditch and wall of the main work were reached; the scaling ladders were brought up and planted by the storming parties; some of the daring spirits, first in the assault, were cast down— killed or wounded; but a lodgment was soon made; streams of heroes followed; all opposition was overcome, and several of our regimental colors flung out from the upper walls, amidst long-continued shouts and cheers, which sent dismay into the capital. No scene could have been more animating or glorious.

Major-General Quitman, nobly supported by Brigadier-Generals Shields and Smith (P. F.), his other officers and men, was up with the part assigned him. Simultaneously with the movement on the west, he had gallantly approached the southeast of the same works over a causeway with cuts and batteries, and defended by an army strongly posted outside, to the east of the works. Those formidable obstacles Quitman had to face, with but little shelter for his troops or space for manœuvring. Deep ditches, flanking the causeway, made it difficult to cross on either side into the adjoining meadows, and these again were intersected by other ditches. Smith and his brigade had been early thrown out to make a sweep to the right, in order to present a front against the enemy's line (outside), and to turn two intervening batteries, near the foot of Chapultepec.

This movement was also intended to support Quitman's storming parties, both on the causeway. The first of these, furnished by Twiggs's division, was commanded in succession by Captain Casey, 2d Infantry, and Captain Paul, 7th Infantry, after Casey had been severely wounded; and the second, originally under the gallant Major Twiggs, Marine Corps, killed, and then Captain Miller, 2d Pennsylvania Volunteers. The storming party, now commanded by Captain Paul, seconded by Captain Roberts of the Rifles, Lieutenant Stewart, and others of the same regiment, Smith's brigade, carried the two batteries in the road, took some guns, with many prisoners, and drove the enemy posted behind in support. The New York and South Carolina Volunteers (Shields's brigade), and the 2d Pennsylvania

Volunteers, all on the left of Quitman's line, together with portions of his storming parties, crossed the meadows in front under a heavy fire, and entered the outer enclosure of Chapultepec just in time to join in the final assault from the west.

Besides Major-Generals Pillow and Quitman, Brigadier-Generals Shields, Smith, and Cadwallader, the following are the officers and corps most distinguished in those brilliant operations: The Voltigeur regiment, in two detachments, commanded respectively by Colonel Andrews and Lieutenant-Colonel Joseph Johnston —the latter mostly in the lead, accompanied by Major Caldwell; Captains Barnard and C. J. Biddle, of the same regiment—the former the first to plant a regimental color, and the latter among the first in the assault; —the storming party of Worth's division, under Captain McKenzie, 2d Artillery, with Lieutenant Selden, 8th Infantry, early on the ladder and badly wounded; Lieutenant Armistead, 6th Infantry, the first to leap into the ditch to plant a ladder; Lieutenant Rogers, of the 4th, and J. P. Smith, of the 5th Infantry—both mortally wounded; the 9th Infantry, under Colonel Ransom, who was killed while gallantly leading that gallant regiment; the 15th Infantry, under Lieutenant-

Colonel Howard and Major Woods, with Captain Chase, whose company gallantly carried the redoubt, midway up the acclivity;—Colonel Clarke's brigade (Worth's division), consisting of the 5th, 8th, and part of the 6th regiments of infantry, commanded respectively by Captain Chapman, Major Montgomery, and Lieutenant Edward Johnson—the latter specially noticed—with Lieutenants Longstreet (badly wounded, advancing, colors in hand), Pickett, and Merchant—the last three of the 8th Infantry;—portions of the United States' Marines, New York, South Carolina, and 2d Pennsylvania Volunteers, which, delayed with their division (Quitman's) by the hot engagement below, arrived just in time to participate in the assault of the heights; particularly a detachment, under Lieutenant Reed, New York Volunteers, consisting of a company of the same, with one of marines; and another detachment, a portion of the storming party (Twiggs's division, serving with Quitman), under Lieutenant Steele, 2d Infantry, after the fall of Lieutenant Gantt, 7th Infantry.

In this connection, it is but just to recall the decisive effect of the heavy batteries, Nos. 1, 2, 3, and 4, commanded by those excellent officers, Captain Drum,

4th Artillery, assisted by Lieutenants Benjamin and Porter of his own company; Captain Brooks and Lieutenant Anderson, 2d Artillery, assisted by Lieutenant Russell, 4th Infantry, a volunteer; Lieutenants Hagner and Stone, of the Ordnance, and Lieutenant Andrews, 3d Artillery — the whole superintended by Captain Huger, Chief of Ordnance with this army, an officer distinguished by every kind of merit. The Mountain Howitzer Battery, under Lieutenant Reno, of the Ordnance, deserves also to be particularly mentioned. Attached to the Voltigeurs, it followed the movements of that regiment, and again won applause.

In adding to the list of individuals of conspicuous merit, I must limit myself to a few of the many names which might be enumerated:—Captain Hooker, Assistant Adjutant-General, who won special applause, successively, in the staff of Pillow and Cadwallader; Lieutenant Lovell, 4th Artillery (wounded), chief of Quitman's staff; Captain Page, Assistant Adjutant-General (wounded), and Lieutenant Hammond, 3d Artillery, both of Shields's staff, and Lieutenant Van Dorn (7th Infantry), Aide-de-Camp to Brigadier-General Smith.

Those operations all occurred on the west, south-east, and heights of Chapultepec. To the north, and at the base of the mound, inaccessible on that side, the 11th Infantry, under Lieutenant-Colonel Hebert, the 14th, under Colonel Trousdale, and Captain Magruder's field battery, 1st Artillery, one section advanced under Lieutenant Jackson, all of Pillow's division, had, at the same time, some spirited affairs against superior numbers, driving the enemy from a battery in the road, and capturing a gun. In these, the officers and corps named gained merited praise. Colonel Trousdale, the commander, though twice wounded, continued on duty until the heights were carried.

Early in the morning of the 13th, I repeated the orders of the night before to Major-General Worth, to be with his division at hand to support the movement of Major-General Pillow from our left. The latter seems soon to have called for that entire division, standing momentarily in reserve, and Worth sent him Colonel Clarke's brigade. The call, if not unnecessary, was at least, from the circumstances, unknown to me at the time; for, soon observing that the very large body of the enemy, in the road in front of Major-General Quitman's right, was receiving reënforcements from the city—less than a mile and a half to the east— I sent instructions to Worth, on our opposite flank, to turn Chapultepec with his division, and to proceed cautiously by the road at its northern base, in order, if not met by very superior numbers, to threaten or to attack in rear that body of the enemy. The movement it was also believed could not fail to distract and to intimidate the enemy generally.

Worth promptly advanced with his remaining brigade — Colonel Garland's—Lieutenant-Colonel C. F. Smith's light battalion, Lieutenant-Colonel Duncan's field battery—all of his division—and three squadrons of dragoons, under Major Sumner, which I had just ordered up to join in the movement.

Having turned the forest on the west, and arriving opposite to the north centre of Chapultepec, Worth came up with the troops in the road, under Colonel Trousdale, and aided, by a flank movement of a part of Garland's brigade, in taking the one-gun breastwork, then under the fire of Lieutenant Jackson's section of Captain Magruder's field battery. Continuing to advance, this division passed Chapultepec, attacking the right of the enemy's line, resting on that road, about the moment of the general retreat consequent upon the capture of the formidable castle and its outworks.

Arriving some minutes later, and mounting to the

top of the castle, the whole field to the east lay plainly under my view.

There are two routes from Chapultepec to the capital—the one on the right entering the same gate, Belén, with the road from the south, *via* Piedad; and the other obliquing to the left, to intersect the great western, or San Cosme road, in a suburb outside of the gate of San Cosme.

Each of these routes (an elevated causeway) presents a double roadway on the sides of an aqueduct of strong masonry, and great height, resting on open arches and massive pillars, which, together, afford fine points both for attack and defence. The sideways of both aqueducts were, moreover, defended by many strong breastworks at the gates, and before reaching them. As we had expected, we found the four tracks unusually dry and solid for the season.

Worth and Quitman were prompt in pursuing the retreating enemy—the former by the San Cosme aqueduct, and the latter along that of Belén. Each had now advanced some hundred yards.

Deeming it all-important to profit by our successes, and the consequent dismay of the enemy, which could not be otherwise than general, I hastened to despatch from Chapultepec, first Clarke's brigade, and then Cadwallader's, to the support of Worth, and gave orders that the necessary heavy guns should follow. Pierce's brigade was, at the same time, sent to Quitman, and in the course of the afternoon I caused some additional siege pieces to be added to his train. Then after designating the 15th Infantry, under Lieu-tenant-Colonel Howard—Morgan, the colonel, had been disabled by a wound at Churubusco—as the garrison of Chapultepec, and giving directions for the care of the prisoners of war, the captured ordnance and ordnance stores, I proceeded to join the advance of Worth, within the suburb, and beyond the turn at the junction of the aqueduct with the great highway from the west to the gate of San Cosme.

At this junction of roads, we first passed one of those formidable systems of city defences, spoken of above, and it had not a gun !—a strong proof, 1. That the enemy had expected us to fail in the attack upon Chapultepec, even if we meant anything more than a feint ; 2. That in either case, we designed, in his belief, to return and double our forces against the southern gates, a delusion kept up by the active demonstrations of Twiggs with the forces posted on that side; and 3. That advancing rapidly from the reduction of Chapultepec, the enemy had not time to shift guns — our previous captures had left him, comparatively, but few—from the southern gates.

Within those disgarnished works, I found our troops engaged in a street fight against the enemy posted in gardens, at windows and on housetops—all flat, with parapets. Worth ordered forward the mountain howitzers of Cadwallader's brigade, preceded by skirmishers and pioneers, with pick-axes and crow-bars, to force windows and doors, or to burrow through walls. The assailants were soon on an equality of position fatal to the enemy. By eight o'clock in the evening, Worth had carried two batteries in this suburb. According to my instructions, he here posted guards and sentinels, and placed his troops under shelter for the night, *within* the San Cosme gate (custom-house.)

I had gone back to the foot of Chapultepec, the point from which the two aqueducts begin to diverge, some hours earlier, in order to be near that new dépôt, and in easy communication with Quitman and Twiggs, as well as with Worth.

From this point I ordered all detachments and stragglers to their respective corps, then in advance;

sent to Quitman additional siege guns, ammunition,
intrenching tools; directed Twiggs's remaining brigade
(Riley's) from Piedad, to support Worth; and Captain
Steptoe's field battery, also at Piedad, to rejoin Quitman's division.

I had been, from the first, well aware that the
western or San Cosme, was the less difficult route to
the centre and conquest of the capital; and therefore
intended that Quitman should only manœuvre and
threaten the Belén or southwestern gate, in order to
favor the main attack by Worth—knowing that the
strong defences at the Belén were directly under the
guns of the much stronger fortress, called *the citadel*,
just within.   Both of these defences of the enemy were
also within easy supporting distance from the San
Angel (or Niño Perdido) and San Antonio gates.
Hence the greater support, in numbers, given to
Worth's movement as the main attack.

Those views I repeatedly, in the course of the day,
communicated to Major-General Quitman; but being
in hot pursuit, gallant himself, and ably supported by
Brigadier-Generals Shields and Smith—Shields badly
wounded before Chapultepec and refusing to retire—as
well as by all the officers and men of the column,

Quitman continued to press forward, under flank and direct fires, carried an intermediate battery of two guns, and then the gate, before two o'clock in the afternoon, but not without proportionate loss, increased by his steady maintenance of that position.

Here, of the heavy battery—4th Artillery—Captain Drum and Lieutenant Benjamin were mortally wounded, and Lieutenant Porter, its third in rank, slightly. The loss of these two most distinguished officers the army will long mourn. Lieutenants I. B. Moragne and William Canty, of the South Carolina Volunteers, also of high merit, fell on the same occasion—besides many of our bravest non-commissioned officers and men, particularly in Captain Drum's veteran company. I cannot in this place, give names or numbers; but full returns of the killed and wounded of all corps, in their recent operations, will accompany this report.

Quitman, within the city, adding several new defences to the position he had won, and sheltering his corps as well as practicable, now awaited the return of daylight under the guns of the formidable citadel, yet to be subdued.

At about four o'clock next morning (September 14),

a deputation of the *ayuntamiento* (city council) waited upon me to report that the Federal Government and the army of Mexico had fled from the capital some three hours before, and to demand terms of capitulation in favor of the church, the citizens, and the municipal authorities. I promptly replied, that I would sign no capitulation; that the city had been virtually in our possession from the time of the lodgments effected by Worth and Quitman the day before; that I regretted the silent escape of the Mexican army; that I should levy upon the city a moderate contribution, for special purposes; and that the American army should come under no terms, not *self*-imposed—such only as its own honor, the dignity of the United States, and the spirit of the age, should, in my opinion, imperiously demand and impose.

For the terms so imposed, I refer the department to subsequent general orders, Nos. 287 and 289 (paragraphs 7, 8, and 9, of the latter), copies of which are herewith enclosed.

At the termination of the interview with the city deputation, I communicated, about daylight, orders to Worth and Quitman to advance slowly and cautiously (to guard against treachery) toward the heart of the city, and to occupy its stronger and more commanding points.   Quitman proceeded to the great *plaza* or square, planted guards, and hoisted the colors of the United States on the national palace—containing the Halls of Congress and Executive apartments of Federal Mexico.   In this grateful service, Quitman might have been anticipated by Worth, but for my express orders, halting the latter at the head of the *Alameda* (a green park), within three squares of that goal of general ambition.

The capital, however, was not taken by any one or two corps, but by the talent, the science, the gallantry, the vigor of this entire army.   In the glorious conquest, *all* had contributed—early and powerfully—the killed, the wounded, and *the fit for duty*—at Vera Cruz, Cerro Gordo, Contreras, San Antonio, Churubusco (three battles), the Molinos del Rey, and Chapultepec—as much as those who fought at the gates of Belén and San Cosme.

Soon after we had entered, and were in the act of occupying the city, a fire was opened upon us from the flat roofs of the houses, from windows and corners of streets, by some two thousand convicts, liberated the night before, by the flying Government—joined by, perhaps, as many Mexican soldiers, who had disbanded themselves and thrown off their uniforms. This unlawful war lasted more than twenty-four hours, in spite of the exertions of the municipal authorities, and was not put down till we had lost many men, including several officers, killed or wounded, and had punished the miscreants. Their objects were to gratify national hatred; and, in the general alarm and confusion, to plunder the wealthy inhabitants—particularly the deserted houses. But families are now generally returning; business of every kind has been resumed, and the city is already tranquil and cheerful, under the admirable conduct (with exceptions very few and trifling) of our gallant troops.

This army has been more disgusted than surprised that, by some sinister process on the part of certain individuals at home, its numbers have been, generally, almost trebled in our public papers—beginning at Washington.

Leaving, as we all feared, inadequate garrisons at Vera Cruz, Perote, and Puebla—with much larger hospitals; and being obliged, most reluctantly, from the same cause (general paucity of numbers) to abandon Jalapa, we marched [August 7–10] from Puebla

23

with only ten thousand seven hundred and thirty-eight rank and file. This number includes the garrison of Jalapa, and the two thousand four hundred and twenty-nine men brought up by Brigadier-General Pierce, August 6.

At Contreras, Churubusco, etc. [August 20], we had but eight thousand four hundred and ninety-seven men engaged—after deducting the garrison of San Augustin (our general dépôt), the intermediate sick and the dead; at the Molinos del Rey (September 8), but three brigades, with some cavalry and artillery—making in all three thousand two hundred and fifty-one men—were in the battle; in the two days—September 12 and 13— our whole operating force, after deducting again the recent killed, wounded, and sick, together with the garrison of Mixcoac (the then general dépôt) and that of Tacubaya, was but seven thousand one hundred and eighty; and, finally, after deducting the new garrison of Chapultepec, with the killed and wounded of the two days, we took possession (September 14) of this great capital with less than six thousand men! And I reassert, upon accumulated and unquestionable evidence, that, in not one of these conflicts, was this army opposed by fewer than three and a half times numbers—in several of them, by a yet greater excess.

I recapitulate our losses since we arrived in the basin of Mexico:

August 19, 20: *Killed*, 137, including 14 officers. *Wounded*, 877, including 62 officers. *Missing* (probably killed), 38 rank and file. *Total*, 1,052. September 8: *Killed*, 116, including 9 officers. *Wounded*, 665, including 49 officers. *Missing*, 18 rank and file. *Total*, 789.

September 12, 13, 14: *Killed*, 130, including 10 officers. *Wounded*, 703, including 68 officers. *Missing*, 29 rank and file. *Total*, 862.

Grand total of losses, 2,703, including 383 officers.

On the other hand, this small force has beaten on the same occasions, in view of their capital, the whole Mexican army, of (at the beginning) thirty-odd thousand men—posted, always, in chosen positions, behind intrenchments, or more formidable defences of nature and art; killed or wounded, of that number, more than seven thousand officers and men; taken 3,730 prisoners, one-seventh officers, including thirteen generals, of whom three had been presidents of this republic; captured more than twenty colors and standards, seventy-five pieces of ordnance, besides fifty-seven wall pieces, twenty thousand small arms,* an immense quantity of shots, shells, powder, etc., etc.

Of that enemy, once so formidable in numbers, appointments, artillery, etc., twenty-odd thousand have disbanded themselves in despair, leaving, as is known, not more than three fragments—the largest about two thousand five hundred—now wandering in different directions, without magazines or a military chest, and living *at free quarters* upon their own people.

General Santa Anna, himself a fugitive, is believed to be on the point of resigning the chief magistracy, and escaping to neutral Guatemala. A new President, no doubt, will soon be declared, and the Federal Congress is expected to reassemble at Queretaro, one hundred and twenty-five miles north of this, on the Zacatecas road, some time in October. I have seen and given safe conduct through this city to several of its members. The Government will find itself without

---

* Besides those in the hands of prisoners. The twenty thousand new muskets (British manufacture) found in the citadel, were used in a novel way. Iron being scarce in the interior, the barrels made excellent shoes for our horses and mules, and the brass cuffs or bands were worked up into spear heads for the color-staffs, and spurs for the cavalry and all mounted officers.

resources; no army, no arsenals, no magazines, and but little revenue, internal or external. Still such is the obstinacy, or rather infatuation, of this people, that it is very doubtful whether the new authorities will dare to sue for peace on the terms which, in the recent negotiations, were made known by our minister

*   *   *   *   *   *   *   *   *

In conclusion, I beg to enumerate, once more, with due commendation and thanks, the distinguished staff officers, general and personal, who, in our last operations in front of the enemy accompanied me, and communicated orders to every point and through every danger. Lieutenant-Colonel Hitchcock, Acting Inspector-General; Major Turnbull and Lieutenant Hardcastle, Topographical Engineers; Major Kirby, Chief Paymaster; Captain Irwin, Chief Quartermaster; Captain Grayson, Chief Commissary; Captain H. L. Scott, Chief in the Adjutant-General's Department; Lieutenant Williams, Aide-de-Camp; Lieutenant Lay, Military Secretary, and Major J. P. Gaines, Kentucky Cavalry, Volunteer Aide-de-Camp. Captain Lee, Engineer, so constantly distinguished, also bore important orders from me (September 13) until he fainted from a wound and the loss of two nights' sleep at the batteries. Lieutenants Beauregard, Stevens, and Tower, all wounded, were employed with the divisions, and Lieutenants G. W. Smith, and G. B. McClellan, with the company of Sappers and Miners. Those five lieutenants of engineers, like their captain, won the admiration of all about them.　The Ordnance officers, Captain Huger, Lieutenants Hagner, Stone, and Reno, were highly effective, and distinguished at the several batteries; and I may add that Captain McKinstry, Assistant Quartermaster, at the close of the operations, executed several important commissions for me as a special volunteer.

Surgeon-General Lawson, and the medical staff generally, were skilful and untiring in and out of fire, in ministering to the numerous wounded.

To illustrate the operations in this basin, I enclose two beautiful drawings, prepared under the directions of Major Turnbull, mostly from actual survey.

I have the honor to be, etc., etc.,

WINFIELD SCOTT.

Hon. Wm. L. Marcy, *Secretary of War.*

The foregoing reports are taken from Ex. Doc. 60 (H. of R. April 28, 1848), beginning at p. 1046.

The aides-de-camp engaged in copying the original sheets as they were written, said to me several times: "Why, General! you have understated the general result." I replied: "Mum! If our countrymen believe what is given, we may be content; whereas if I tell the whole truth, they may say—'It is all a romance.'"

Under a brilliant sun, I entered the city at the head of the cavalry, cheered by Worth's division of regulars drawn up in the order of battle in the Alameda, and by Quitman's division of volunteers in the grand plaza between the National Palace and the Cathedral—all the bands playing, in succession, *Hail Columbia,* *Washington's March,* *Yankee Doodle,* *Hail to the Chief,* etc. Even the inhabitants, catching the enthusiasm of the moment, filled the windows and lined the parapets, cheering the cavalcade as it passed at the gallop.

On entering the Palace, the following order was early published to the army:

<table>
<tr><td>GENERAL ORDERS.
No. 286.</td><td>HEADQUARTERS OF THE ARMY,
NATIONAL PALACE OF MEXICO,
September, 1847.</td></tr>
</table>

The General-in-Chief calls upon his brethren in arms to return, both in public and private worship, thanks and gratitude to God for the signal triumphs which they have recently achieved for their country.

Beginning with the 19th of August, and ending the 14th instant, this army has gallantly fought its way through the fields and forts of Contreras, San Antonio, Churubusco, Molino del Rey, Chapultepec, and the gates of San Cosme and Tacubaya or Belén, into the capital of Mexico.

When the very limited numbers who have performed those brilliant deeds shall have become known, the world will be astonished, and our own countrymen filled with joy and admiration.

But all is not yet done. The enemy, though scattered and dismayed, has still many fragments of his late army hovering about us, and, aided by an exasperated population, he may again reunite in treble our numbers, and fall upon us to advantage if we rest inactive on the security of past victories.

Compactness, vigilance, and discipline are, therefore, our only securities. Let every good officer and man look to those cautions and enjoin them upon all others.

By command of Major-General Scott.

H. L. SCOTT,

A. A.-General.

The day after entering the capital the British consul-general called to ask for an escort of cavalry, and a written passport in behalf of the young and beautiful wife of President Santa Anna, to enable her to follow her husband. Both were, of course, promised; but, finally, she only accepted the passport, deeming that a sufficient protection.

At first, I said to the consul I would do myself the honor to make my respects to the fair lady in person; but reflecting a moment, I gave up the visit, as, under the circumstances, it might by others be regarded as a vaunt on my part.

CHAPTER XXXIII.

BRILLIANT ALLUSION TO THE CAMPAIGN — RETALIATORY
MEASURES — MARTIAL LAW — SAFEGUARDS — PROCLA-
MATION—DEFENCE OF PUEBLA.

So ended the second conquest of Mexico, which has
been beautifully, though extravagantly alluded to by a
distinguished person — Sir Henry Bulwer, sometime
British Minister accredited to this country. At the
celebration of St. Andrew's Day, New York, November 30, 1850, Sir Henry being called up, brought into
parallelism two British subjects with two Americans—
thus :

" All [present] were children of St. Andrew, or to
say the least, nephews of St. George. All were birds

of the same feather, though they might roost on different trees; members of the same family, though they might be adopted by different lands. .Even their national history was individualized by the same names. Who was the first martyr to religious liberty in Scotland? One PATRICK HAMILTON (if he did not mistake), who was burnt in front of the College of St. Salvador, in Edinburgh, by an archbishop of St. Andrew's. Who was the foremost amongst the wisest, because the most moderate of the early champions of civil liberty in America? ALEXANDER HAMILTON, who perished beneath the cliffs of Weehawken, also a victim to a barbarous custom and the courage with which he vindicated his opinions. Nor was this all. Passing from the royal house of Hamilton to the princely house of Buccleuch, might he not say, in later and more recent times, that if Waverley and Guy Mannering had made the name of Scott immortal, on one side of the Atlantic, Cerro Gordo and Churubusco had equally immortalized it on the other. If the novelist had given the garb of truth to fiction, had not the warrior given to truth the air of romance?"—*National Intelligencer, December* 4, 1850.

No doubt the conquest so splendidly alluded to by the orator, was mainly due to the science and prowess of the army. But valor and professional science could not alone have dictated a treaty of peace with double our numbers, in double the time, and with double the loss of life, without the measures of conciliation perseveringly adhered to, the perfect discipline and order maintained in the army. Those measures heretofore alluded to are here recorded:

The *martial law order*, often alluded to above, page 392, etc., was first published at Tampico, February 19, 1847. The second edition was reprinted at Vera Cruz, the third at Puebla, and the last as follows:

<table>
<tr><td>GENERAL ORDERS,
No. 287.</td><td>HEADQUARTERS OF THE ARMY,
NATIONAL PALACE OF MEXICO,
September 17, 1847.</td></tr>
</table>

The General-in-Chief republishes, with important additions, the General Orders, No. 20, of February 19, 1847 (declaring MARTIAL LAW*), to govern all who may be concerned.*

1. It is still to be apprehended that many grave offences, not provided for in the Act of Congress " es-

tablishing rules and articles for the government of the armies of the United States," approved April 10, 1806, may again be committed—by, or upon, individuals of those armies, in Mexico, pending the existing war between the two Republics. Allusion is here made to offences, any one of which, if committed within the United States or their organized Territories, would, of course, be tried and severely punished by the ordinary or civil courts of the land.

2. Assassination, murder, poisoning, rape, or the attempt to commit either; malicious stabbing or maiming; malicious assault and battery, robbery, theft; the wanton desecration of churches, cemeteries or other religious edifices and fixtures; the interruption of religious ceremonies, and the destruction, except by order of a superior officer, of public or private property; are such offences.

3. The good of the service, the honor of the United States and the interests of humanity, imperiously demand that every crime, enumerated above, should be severely punished.

4. But the written code, as above, commonly called the *rules and articles of war*, does not provide for the punishment of any *one* of those crimes, even when com-

mitted by individuals of the army upon the persons or property of other individuals of the same, except in the very restricted case in the 9th of those articles; nor for like outrages, committed by the same class of individuals, upon the persons or property of a hostile country, except very partially, in the 51st, 52d, and 55th articles; and the same code is absolutely silent as to all injuries which may be inflicted upon individuals of the army, or their property, against the laws of war, by individuals of a hostile country.

5. It is evident that the 99th article, independent of any reference to the restriction in the 87th, is wholly nugatory in reaching any one of those high crimes.

6. For all the offences, therefore, enumerated in the second paragraph above, which may be committed abroad—in, by, or upon the army, a supplemental code is absolutely needed.

7. That *unwritten* code is *Martial Law*, as an addition to the *written* military code, prescribed by Congress in the rules and articles of war, and which unwritten code, all armies, in hostile countries, are forced to adopt—not only for their own safety, but for the protection of the unoffending inhabitants and their property, about the theatres of military operations,

against injuries, on the part of the army, contrary to the laws of war.

8. From the same supreme necessity, martial law is hereby declared as a supplemental code in, and about, all cities, towns, camps, posts, hospitals, and other places which may be occupied by any part of the forces of the United States, in Mexico, and in, and about, all columns, escorts, convoys, guards, and detachments, of the said forces, while engaged in prosecuting the existing war in, and against the said republic, and while remaining within the same.

9. Accordingly, every crime, enumerated in paragraph No. 2, above, whether committed—1. By any inhabitant of Mexico, sojourner or traveller therein, upon the person or property of any individual of the United States forces, retainer or follower of the same; 2. By any individual of the said forces, retainer or follower of the same, upon the person or property of any inhabitant of Mexico, sojourner or traveller therein; or 3. By any individual of the said forces, retainer or follower of the same, upon the person or property of any other individual of the said forces, retainer or follower of the same—shall be duly tried and punished under the said supplemental code.

10. For this purpose it is ordered, that all offenders, in the matters aforesaid, shall be promptly seized, confined, and reported for trial, before *military commissions*, to be duly appointed as follows:

11. Every military commission, under this order, will be appointed, governed, and limited, as nearly as practicable, as prescribed by the 65th, 66th, 67th, and 97th, of the said rules and articles of war, and the proceedings of such commissions will be duly recorded, in writing, reviewed, revised, disapproved or approved, and the sentences executed—all, as near as may be, as in the cases of the proceedings and sentences of courts martial, *provided,* that no military commission shall try any case clearly cognizable by any court martial, and *provided,* also, that no sentence of a military commission shall be put in execution against any individual belonging to this army, which may not be, according to the nature and degree of the offence, as established by evidence, in conformity with known punishments, in like cases, in some one of the States of the United States of America.

12. The sale, waste or loss of ammunition, horses, arms, clothing or accoutrements, by soldiers, is punishable under the 37th and 38th articles of war. Any

Mexican or resident or traveller, in Mexico, who shall purchase of any American soldier, either horse, horse equipments, arms, ammunition, accoutrements or clothing, shall be tried and severely punished, by a military commission, as above.

13. The administration of justice, both in civil and criminal matters, through the ordinary courts of the country, shall nowhere and in no degree, be interrupted by any officer or soldier of the American forces, except,

1. In cases to which an officer, soldier, agent, servant, or follower of the American army may be a party; and

2. In *political* cases—that is, prosecutions against other individuals on the allegations that they have given friendly information, aid or assistance to the American forces.

14. For the ease and safety of both parties, in all cities and towns occupied by the American army, a Mexican police shall be established and duly harmonized with the military police of the said forces.

15. This splendid capital—its churches and religious worship; its convents and monasteries; its inhabitants and property are, moreover, placed under the special safeguard of the faith and honor of the American army.

16. In consideration of the foregoing protection, a

contribution of $150,000 is imposed on this capital, to be paid in four weekly instalments of thirty-seven thousand five hundred dollars ($37,500) each, beginning on Monday next, the 20th instant, and terminating on Monday, the 11th of October.

17. The Ayuntamiento, or corporate authority of the city, is specially charged with the collection and payment of the several instalments.

18. Of the whole contributions to be paid over to this army, twenty thousand dollars shall be appropriated to the purchase of *extra* comforts for the wounded and sick in hospital; ninety thousand dollars ($90,000) to the purchase of blankets and shoes for gratuitous distribution among the rank and file of the army, and forty thousand dollars ($40,000) reserved for other necessary military purposes.

19. This order will be read at the head of every company of the United States' forces, serving in Mexico, and translated into Spanish for the information of Mexicans.

By command of Major-General Scott.

H. L. SCOTT,

A. A.-General.

The following printed regulations, among others, were in the hands of the whole army, and are here extracted as subsidiary to the martial law order:

As a *special* security, any general-in-chief, general of an army corps, or division, is authorized to give *safeguards* to hospitals, public establishments of instruction, of religion, or of charity, also to mills, post offices, and the like. They may, further, give them to individuals whom it is the particular interest of the army to protect.

"Whosoever, belonging to the armies of the United States, employed in foreign parts, shall force a safeguard, shall suffer death" (54th article of war).

A safeguard may consist of one or more men of fidelity and firmness, generally non-effective sergeants or corporals, furnished with a printed or written paper, purporting the character and object of the guard, or it may consist of such paper only, delivered to the inhabitant of the country, whose house, etc., it is designed to protect. Disrespect to such a paper, when produced, constitutes the offence, and incurs the penalty mentioned in the article, etc., above cited.

The men left with a safeguard may require of the

persons for whose benefit they are so left, reasonable subsistence and lodging; and the neighboring inhabit-. ants will be held responsible, by the army, for any violence done them.

The bearers of a safeguard left by one corps, may be replaced by the corps that follows; and if the country be evacuated, they will be recalled; or they may be instructed to wait for the arrival of the enemy, and demand of him a safe conduct to the outposts of the army.

The following form will be used:

SAFEGUARD.

By authority of Major-Gen. —— (*Or Brigadier-Gen.* ——).

The person, the property, and the family of—— (or such a college, and the persons and things belonging to it; such a mill, etc.), *are placed under the safeguard of the United States. To offer any violence or injury to them is expressly forbidden ; on the contrary, it is ordered that safety and protection be given to him, or them, in case of need.*

Done at the Headquarters of ——, this —— day of ——, 18—.

Forms of safeguards ought to be printed in blank,

headed by the article of war relative thereto, and held ready to be filled up, as occasions may offer. A duplicate, etc., in each case, might be affixed to the houses, or edifices, to which they relate.

But the crowning act of conciliation was the proclamation that I issued at Jalapa, May 11, 1847, indignantly denying the "calumnies put forth by the [Mexican] press in order to excite hostility against us," and confidently appealing to "the clergy, civil authorities, and inhabitants of all the places we have occupied." "The army of the United States," I continued, "respects, and will ever respect private property and persons, and the property of the Mexican Church. Woe to him who does not, where we are!"—*Ex. Doc. No.* 60, *H. of R.*, 30*th Congress*, 1*st Session*. Brevet Major-General Worth, though hostile to me, wrote from the advanced position, Puebla—"It was most fortunate that I got hold of one copy of your proclamation. I had a third edition struck off, and am now with hardly a copy on hand. It takes admirably and my doors are crowded for it."

* * * * * * * * *

" It has produced more decided effects than all the blows from Palo Alto to Cerro Gordo."—*Ibid*, p. 967.

Retiring from the capital, Santa Anna collected several fragments of his late army and laid siege to Puebla—the garrison of which being considerably less than was intended; for, although, on advancing from that city I gave the strictest orders that all convalescents as well as the sick should be left behind, about six hundred of the former imposed themselves upon their medical and company officers as entirely restored to health. For stationary or garrison duty they would have been fully qualified, but proved a burden to the advancing columns; for they soon began to break down and to creep into the subsistence wagons faster than these were lightened by the consumption of the troops.

The siege was prosecuted with considerable vigor for twenty-eight days, and nobly repulsed by our able and distinguished commander, Colonel Childs, with his gallant but feeble garrison, at all points and at every assault. During those arduous and protracted operations, the glory of our arms was nobly supported by officers and men. Colonel Childs specially commends by name—and no doubt justly—the skill, zeal, and prowess of Lieutenant-Colonel Black and Captain Small, both of the Pennsylvania Volunteers; the highly accomplished Captain [now Professor] Kendrick, United

States 4th Artillery, chief of that arm, and Captain Miller, of the same regiment; Lieutenant Laidley, of the Ordnance; Captain Rowe of the 9th Infantry, and Lieutenant T. G. Rhett, A. C. S. Captain W. C. De Hart (Artillery), and Lieutenant-Governor of Puebla, though in feeble heath, conducted a sortie with success, and was otherwise distinguished. Death soon after deprived the service of this accomplished officer.

CHAPTER XXXIV.

EARLY in the campaign I began to receive letters
from Washington, urging me to support the army by
forced contributions. Under the circumstances, this
was an impossibility. The population was sparse. We
had no party in the country, and had to encounter the
hostility of both religion and race. All Mexicans, at
first, regarded us as infidels and robbers. Hence there
was not among them a farmer, a miller, or dealer in
subsistence, who would not have destroyed whatever
property he could not remove beyond our reach sooner
than allow it to be seized without compensation. For

the first day or two we might, perhaps, have seized current subsistence within five miles of our route; but by the end of a week the whole army must have been broken up into detachments and scattered far and wide over the country, skirmishing with *rancheros* and regular troops, for the means of satisfying the hunger of the day. Could invaders, so occupied, have conquered Mexico?

The war being virtually over, I now gave attention to a system of finance for the support of the army and to stimulate overtures of peace. The subject required extensive inquiries and careful elaboration. My intention was to raise the first year about twelve millions of dollars, with the least possible pressure on the industry and wealth of the country, with an increase to fifteen millions in subsequent years. The plan is given at large, in seven papers (four reports and three orders). See *Ex. Doc. No.* 60, *H. of R.*, 30*th Congress*, 1*st Session*, p. 1046, and following. The orders are here omitted and the finance details, contained in the four reports, also.

Report No. 40.

HEADQUARTERS OF THE ARMY, }
MEXICO, *December* 17, 1847. }

SIR:

The troop of Louisiana horse, under Captain Fair-child, that so handsomely escorted up from Vera Cruz Mr. Doyle, the British Chargé d'Affaires, being about to return to its station, I avail myself of the opportunity to write to the department.

I invite attention to my order, No. 376, and particularly to its seventh paragraph—import and export duties. Since its publication, I have seen in a slip, cut from a Vera Cruz newspaper (received here by a merchant), what purports to be a letter, dated the 17th ultimo, from the department to me on the same subject.

* * * * * * * * *

Major - General Butler's and Lieutenant - Colonel Johnston's columns will he here to-day, to-morrow, and the next day; and in a week I propose to despatch one column to San Luis de Potosi. When, or whether, I shall have a sufficient independent force for Zacate-cas, is yet, to me, quite uncertain. The San Luis column, with a view to Tampico, ánd in part to Zacatecas, is the more important, and may be enlarged to, perhaps, seven thousand men.

The following distances from the Mexican official itineraries may be useful: From the capital to Queretaro, is 57 leagues, or 142 miles; thence to Zacatecas, 282 miles—the two distances making 424. From the capital to San Luis, is 113 leagues, or 382 miles (Queretaro may be avoided), and, in continuance by that route, 260 miles to Tampico, or 134 to Zacatecas. Thus, from Mexico, *via* San Luis, to Tampico, is 642 miles, and to Zacatecas, 516; whereas, the distance from Zacatecas to Tampico is but 398. Zacatecas, therefore, may be advantageously reached, or its trade opened with Tampico, *via* San Luis. The difficulty is, to occupy the state capitals of Guanajuato, etc., without passing through and including Queretaro, the temporary capital of the Federal Government; and I am reluctant to disturb that Government whilst it continues intent on a peace with us, without further knowledge of the views at Washington on the subject. That information I hope soon to receive; and, if in favor of covering the country, to hear of the approach of reënforcements behind the column of Brigadier-

General Marshall, now I suppose, as far advanced as Jalapa.

> I have the honor to be, etc., etc.,
>
> WINFIELD SCOTT.

Hon. Secretary of War.

Report No. 41.

> Headquarters of the Army,
> Mexico, *December 25, 1847.*

Sir :

As I had apprehended (in Report No. 37), Lieutenant-Colonel Johnston's train has returned without one blanket, coat, jacket, or pair of pantaloons, the small dépôt at Vera Cruz having been exhausted by the troops under Generals Patterson, Butler, and Marshall, respectively, all fresh from home or the Brazos, and, as in the case of other arrivals, since June, without clothing! The regiments that came with me must, therefore, remain naked, or be supplied with very inferior garments, of every color and at high prices, as we may possibly be able to find the poor materials, and cause them to be made up here. This disappointment may delay any distant expedition for many weeks; for some of the new volunteers are already calling for essential articles of clothing.

Referring again to former letters on the subject, I beg leave to add that every old regiment forwarded, more than a twelvemonth ago, its usual annual requisition for clothing, which has never arrived, or it has been issued as above. With excessive labor I had brought the old regiments—volunteers as well as regulars—favored by our long and necessary halts at Vera Cruz, Jalapa, and Puebla, to respectable degrees of discipline, instruction, conduct, and economy. The same intolerable work, at general headquarters, is to be perpetually renewed, or all the credit heretofore acquired by this army for moral conduct, as well as skill and prowess in the field, will be utterly lost by new arrivals, and there is now no hope of bringing up to the proper standard distant posts and detachments. These cannot be governed by any written code of orders or instructions, sent from a distance. I do not mean to accuse the reënforcements, generally, of deficiency in valor, patriotism, or moral character. Far from it; but among all new levies, of whatever denomination, there are always a few miscreants in every hundred, enough, without *discipline*, to disgrace the entire mass, and what is infinitely worse—the *country* that employs them. My daily distresses under this head weigh me to the earth.

I am about to send a detachment, the 9th Infantry, under Colonel Withers, to Pachuca, near the great mines of Real del Monte, some fifty miles to the north-east. There is an assay office at Pachuca, to which a large amount of silver bullion is soon to be brought, and if we have not troops present, the Federal officers of Mexico will seize the assay duties to our loss. I shall send another detachment in a few days to occupy Toluca, the capital of this State, with the general object of securing the contribution claimed for our military chest.—See General Orders, No. 376, paragraph 5. I am nearly ready to publish the details promised in the tenth paragraph of that order. I have found them very difficult to obtain and to methodize.

There will, I apprehend, be no difficulty in collecting at the assay offices and mints within our reach the ordinary internal dues on the precious metals. As to other internal dues and taxes (not abolished by my order, No. 376), I propose to find the net amount paid, to the Federal Government, for example, by the State of Vera Cruz, for 1843, and to assess that sum, in mass, upon the State, to be paid into our military chest, a twelfth at the end of every month, by the State Government, and so of the other States which are or may be occupied by our troops. Each State will be required to collect the amount claimed, according to the Federal assessment for the year 1843, under certain penalties, which may be the seizure, without payment, of the supplies needed for the support of the occupation, and particularly the property of the State functionaries, Legislative and Executive, with the imprisonment of their persons, etc., etc., etc. The fear is, those··functionaries may abdicate, and leave the States without Governments. In such event, the like penalties will be, so far as practicable, enforced.

The success of the system—on the details of which I am now, with ample materials, employed—depends on our powers of conciliation. With steady troops I should not doubt the result; but the great danger lies in the want of that quality on the part of the new reënforcements, including the recruits of the old regiments. The average number of disorders and crimes, always committed by undisciplined men, with inexperienced officers, may destroy the best-concerted plans, by exasperating the inhabitants, and rendering the war, on their part, national, interminable, and desperate.

It will be perceived that I do not propose to seize the ordinary State or city revenues; as that would, in my humble judgment, be to make war on civilization; as no community can escape absolute anarchy without civil government, and all government must have some revenue for its support. I shall take care, however, to see that the means collected within any particular State or city for that purpose are moderate and reasonable.

It cannot be doubted that there is a considerable party in this country in favor of annexing it entire to the United States. How far that desire may be reciprocated at home, I know not, and it would be impertinent in a soldier to inquire. I am here (whilst I remain) to execute the military orders of my Government. But, as a soldier, I suppose it to be my duty to offer a suggestion on the subject, founded on professional and local knowledge, that may not occur to the minds of statesmen generally.

Annexation and military occupation would be, if we maintain the annexation, one and the same thing, as to the amount of force to be employed by us; for if, after the formal act, by treaty or otherwise, we should withdraw our troops, it cannot be doubted that all Mexico, or rather the active part thereof, would again relapse into a permanent state of revolution, beginning with one *against* annexation. The great mass of this people have always been passive under every form of government that has prevailed in the country, and the turbulent minority, divided into *ins* and *outs*, particularly the military demagogues, are equally incapable of self-government, and delight in nothing but getting power by revolution, and abusing that power when obtained.

I still entertain the belief that propositions, looking to a peace, will be submitted by the incoming Government here, in all the next month; but that any concession of boundaries, satisfactory to the United States, would, on the withdrawment of our forces, create a revolt, or the overthrow of that Government, with a nullification of the treaty, I hold to be events more than probable. In the mean time it would be highly advantageous to me, officially, to have an early intimation of the views of our Government as to the terms of a treaty that would now be satisfactory, only to prevent

24*

a wrong distribution of the troops in respect to those unknown views.

I have received no acknowledged communication from the Department. The letter of the 17th ultimo, published, as I have heretofore mentioned, in a Vera Cruz newspaper, has not come to hand, but I am daily expecting a mail up from that city.

> I have the honor to be, etc., etc.,
>
> WINFIELD SCOTT.

Hon. Secretary of War.

Report No. 42.

> Headquarters of the Army,
> Mexico, *January* 6, 1848.

Sir:

Nothing of interest has occurred since my report of the 26th ultimo; not even the arrival of a mail; but a private conveyance brought up yesterday a letter from Brigadier-General Marshall, representing that he was at Jalapa the 22d ultimo, with a column of troops (number not given), one half of whom were on the sick report, with measles and diarrhœa, and that he had sent back his train to Vera Cruz for medicines and other supplies. He gave no day for the recommencement of his march.

The number on the sick report, in this basin, is also great. In a total of 14,964, we have only 11,162 "for duty." The measles are rife among the new volunteers.

Colonel Withers, with the 9th Infantry, occupied Pachuca, quietly, more than a week ago. Brigadier-General Cadwallader, with the remainder of his brigade, will march for Lerma and Toluca (State capital, thirty-eight miles off, in a direction opposite to Pachuca) to-day. The general object in occupying the three cities is to commence levying the assessments for the last month, and, through them, to enforce peace. Please see copies of General Orders, Nos. 395–8, herewith. (Giving the finance details promised in Order, No. 376.)

The tobacco monopoly I have thought it necessary to abolish. It would be worthless without a prohibition of the plant at the custom houses, and I doubted whether our Government, considering the interests of some five of our own tobacco-growing States, would prohibit the importation. Again, to protect the monopoly, including licenses to cultivators, would require a host of excise men. Probably a reasonable duty on importation will give larger net receipts for a year or two than could be derived in that time from any monopoly however strictly enforced.

Like difficulties in management caused me to relinquish to the Mexican States, respectively, the stamped-paper and playing-card monopolies. More than a substitute will be found in the quadrupling of the direct assessments on the States.

From the want of sufficient numbers to send, at once, columns of five thousand men each to Zacatecas and San Luis de Potosi, respectively, I next proposed to despatch to the latter place a force of seven thousand, which would be sufficient to open the channel of commerce between Tampico and Zacatecas, a distance of three hundred and ninety-four miles, and, by the operation, double, perhaps, the receipts at that seaport, as well as the interior dues on the precious metals. The commercial wealth of Durango would soon fall into the same channel. But assuming seven thousand men as the minimum force for this neighborhood, including the capital, Chapultepec, Pachuca, Lerma, and Toluca, I am obliged to wait for further reënforcements to make up the one column for San Luis. The delay of Brigadier-General Marshall, who had been expected daily for nearly a week, is, therefore, quite a vexatious disappointment. Possibly before his arrival (should the measles here have earlier subsided), I may risk a column of five thousand men, leaving, for a time, two intermediate-posts vacant, and instruct the commander (Major-General Butler) to take into his sphere of operation a part of the forces belonging to the base of the Rio Grande. A detachment moving upon Tula, and, perhaps, leaving Victoria to the left, might coöperate very advantageously with the forces at the new centre, San Luis, and without endangering the line of Monterey, in which direction, it is supposed, the Mexicans cannot have any formidable number of organized troops. To concert the double movement, by correspondence, would be the principal difficulty; but ample discretion would be allowed in my general instructions.

Many of the States of this republic, on account of their remoteness from the common centre, sparseness of population, and inability to pay more than a trifle in the way of contributions, are not worth being occupied. Their influence on the question of peace or war is, proportionally, inconsiderable. As reënforcements arrive, I shall therefore endeavor to occupy only the more populous and wealthy States.

Most of the mints (all but two, I learn) have been farmed by foreigners for terms of years (unexpired), on the payment of large sums in advance. The principal mint (here) is in hands of the British Consul-General, who paid down about $200,000 in February last for the term of ten years, and contracted to pay, currently, one *per centum* on the amount of coinage. I suppose myself bound to respect such contracts until otherwise instructed. Other mints pay, I am informed, one and a half *per centum* on the money turned out. Hence a direction in General Orders, No. 395, to examine the contracts between the Mexican Government and the several mints. Those not under contract will be assessed as heretofore.

By two conveyances I am expecting mails up from Vera Cruz in two and four days. I am anxious to receive the views of the Department on several points of importance to me in this command.

The new Federal Executive and Congress are, as yet, not installed. Both, it is believed, will be strongly inclined to a peace.

I have the honor, etc., etc.,

Hon. Secretary of War.   WINFIELD SCOTT.

Report No. 43.

HEADQUARTERS OF THE ARMY,
MEXICO, *January* 13, 1848.

SIR:

I have not had a line from any public office at Washington of a date later than October 26.

The spy company has returned from Vera Cruz; but it seems that despatches for me had been intrusted to a special messenger (I suppose from Washington), who, after a delay of many days at Perote, came up with the company to Puebla, where he again stopped and retained all my letters.

Brigadier-General Cadwallader has quietly occupied Toluca and Lerma. As was known, the State Government had retired (thirteen leagues) to Sultepec. The general has invited that Government to provide for the payment of the assessment upon the State; but there has not been yet time to receive a reply.

Some days since, Colonel Wynkoop, of the 1st Pennsylvania Volunteers, tendered his services to go, with a few men, to seize the guerilla priest, Jarauta, at the head of a small band that has long been the terror of all peaceable Mexicans within his reach, and who has frequently had skirmishes with our detachments. The colonel having missed that object, heard that General Valencia and staff were at a distant hacienda, and by hard riding in the night, succeeded in capturing that general and a colonel of his staff. I consider this handsome service worthy of being recorded.

Colonel Hays, with a detachment of Texan Rangers, returned last night from a distant expedition in search of the robber priest. In a skirmish, without loss on his part, he killed some eight of Jarauta's men, and thinks that the priest was carried off among the many wounded.

The spy company, coming up from Vera Cruz, had also a very successful affair with a large party of the enemy, and captured some forty prisoners, including three generals.

The second train, now out from Vera Cruz eleven days, was, as I learn by the enclosed correspondence, attacked by a numerous body of the enemy, and suffered a loss that looks like a disaster—the first that we have sustained; but further details are needed.

I have the honor, etc., etc.,

WINFIELD SCOTT.

Hon. Secretary of War.

Report No. 44.

HEADQUARTERS OF THE ARMY,
MEXICO, *February* 2, 1848.

SIR:

Since my last report (January 13), I have received from the War Office letters dated November 8 and 17, and December 14.

My orders, Nos. 362, 376, and 395 of the last year, and 15 of the present (heretofore forwarded), will exhibit the system of finance I have established for the parts of the country occupied by this army.

It will be seen that the export duties on coins, and the prohibition of the export of bars, varies materially from your instructions of November 17, acknowledged above. I hope, for the reasons suggested in my report, No. 40 (December 17), the President may be induced to adopt my views in respect to the precious metals.

I am without reports from commanders of departments below, on the progress made in collecting the direct assessments under my orders and circulars. The *ayuntamiento* (city council) of the capital has charged itself with the payment, on account of the Federal district, of $400,000, of the $668,332 per year, imposed on the State of Mexico, and arrangements are in progress to meet that engagement. Two months are now due. Brigadier-General Cadwallader, at Toluca, hopes soon to begin to collect, through the *ayuntamiento* of that city, a large part of the remainder of the monthly assessments, and I have sent Colonel Clarke with a small brigade to Cueruavaca (some forty-three miles south, on the Acapulco road), to complete the same collection.

The *war of masses* having ended with the capture of this city, the *war of detail*, including the occupation of the country, and the collection of revenue, requires a large additional force, as I suggested in my despatch, No. 34.

I see that I am, at Washington, supposed to have at my command more than thirty thousand men. Including the forces at Tampico, Vera Cruz, on the line thence, and in this neighborhood, our total does not exceed twenty-four thousand eight hundred and sixteen. Deducting the indispensable garrisons and the sick, I have not left a disposable force for distant expeditions of more than four thousand five hundred men, and I do not hear of the approach of any considerable reënforcement. Seven thousand men I deem the *minimum* number necessary to open the important line from Durango, through Zacatecas and San Luis, to Tampico. Premising that I find it impossible to obtain from the volunteers, at a distance, regular returns, I send an approximate estimate of all the forces under my immediate orders. The numbers, among the volunteers, afflicted with the measles and mumps, in this vicinity, continue to be very great, and the erysipelas is common among all the corps.

I write in haste by the express who carries *the project* of a treaty that Mr. Trist has, at the moment, signed with Mexican commissioners. If accepted, I hope to receive, as early as practicable, instructions respecting the evacuation of this country; the disposition to be made of wagons, teams, cavalry, and artillery horses; the points in the United States to which I shall direct the troops respectively, etc., etc. (I have not yet read the treaty, except in small part.) In the same contingency, if not earlier recalled (and I understand my recall has been demanded by two of my juniors!!), I hope to receive instructions to allow me to return to the United States, as soon as I may deem the public service will permit, charging some other general officer with completing the evacuation, which ought, if practicable, to be finished before the return of the *vomito;* say early in May.

In about forty days I may receive an acknowledg ment of this report. By that time, if the treaty be not accepted, I hope to be sufficiently reënforced to open the commercial line between Zacatecas and Tampico. The occupation of Queretaro, Guanajuato, and Guada-lajura would be the next in importance, and some of the ports of the Pacific, the third. Meanwhile, the col-lection of internal dues on the precious metals, and the direct assessments, shall be continued.

I enclose a letter from Commodore Shubrick, and have the honor to remain, etc., etc.,

WINFIELD SCOTT.

Hon. Secretary of War.

Report No. 45.

Headquarters of the Army,
Mexico, *February* 9, 1848.

Sir:

I have received no communication from the War Department, or the Adjutant - General's Office, since my last report (No. 44), dated the 2d instant; but slips from newspapers and letters from Washington have come to interested parties here, representing, I learn, that the President has determined to place me before a court, for daring to enforce necessary discipline in this army against certain of its high officers! I make only a passing comment upon these unofficial announcements; learning with pleasure, through the same sources, that I am to be superseded by Major-General Butler. Perhaps, after trial, I may be permitted to return to the United States. My poor services with this most gallant army are at length to be requited as I have long been led to expect they would be.

I have the honor, etc., etc.,

WINFIELD SCOTT.

Hon. Secretary of War.

CHAPTER XXXV.

A censure of Mr. Jay, on my conduct at Vera Cruz,
is noticed above, at page 428. Another occurs in his
book (*Review of the Mexican War*), page 207. Considering the gravity of his character, this censure also
demands a passing notice.

Some three months after entering the capital of
Mexico I issued an order declaring:

"The highways used, or about to be used, by the
American troops, being still infested in many parts by
those atrocious bands called *guerillas* or *rancheros*,
who, under instructions from the late Mexican authorities, continue to violate every rule of warfare observed

by civilized nations, it has become necessary to announce to all the views and instructions of general headquarters on the subject." And it was added: "No quarter will be given to known murderers or robbers, whether guerillas or rancheros, and whether serving under [obsolete] commissions or not. Offenders of this character, accidentally falling into the hands of American troops [that is, without knowing their character], will be momentarily held as prisoners, that is, not put to death without due solemnity," meaning (and it was so prescribed) a trial by a council of three officers. This order Mr. Jay denounces as harsh or cruel.

Now in charity, Mr. Jay must be supposed to have been ignorant of what was universally known in Mexico, that the outlaws, denounced in the order, never made a prisoner, but invariably put to death every accidental American straggler, wounded or sick man, that fell into their hands—whether he was left by accident, in hospital or in charge of a Mexican family. And Mr. Jay, no doubt, must have known that it is a universal right of war, not to give quarter to an enemy that puts to death all who fall into his hands.

Some time before the date of that order, Mr Trist,

our peace commissioner, long my guest, reopened negotiations at the instance of the Mexican Government, in
the hope of terminating hostilities; but early in the
negotiations he was recalled. I encouraged him, nevertheless, to finish the good work he had begun. The
Mexican commissioners, knowing of the recall, hesitated.
On application, I encouraged them also, giving it as my
confident belief that any treaty Mr. Trist might sign
would be duly ratified at Washington.

Mr. Trist approached me at Jalapa under circumstances quite adverse to harmony. We had known
each other very slightly at Washington, with, from
accident, evident feelings of mutual dislike. With his
arrival I received the most reliable information from
Washington, that his well-known prejudice against me
had had much weight in his appointment; and I remembered that, on taking leave of the President, he
told me he intended or hoped to send to reside at headquarters with me, the very eminent statesman, Silas
Wright, as peace commissioner, with an associate—
leaving me half at liberty to believe, I might, myself,
be the other commissioner. What could have been more
natural? Writing to the Secretary of War on this subject, May 20, 1847, from Jalapa, I said:

" The Hon. Mr. Benton has publicly declared, that if the law had passed making him General-in-Chief of the United States armies in Mexico, either as lieutenant-general or as junior major-general over seniors, the power would have been given him not only of agreeing to an armistice (which would, of course, have appertained to his position), but the much higher one of concluding a treaty of peace; and it will be remembered also, that in my letter to Major-General Taylor, dated June 12, 1846, written at your instance [etc.], his power to agree to an armistice was merely adverted to in order to place upon it certain limitations. I understand your letter to me of the 14th ultimo, as not only taking from me, the commander of an army, under the most critical circumstances, all voice or advice in agreeing to a truce with the enemy, but as an attempt to place me under the military command of Mr. Trist; for you tell me that 'should he make known to you in writing, that the contingency had occurred in consequence of which the President is willing that further active military operations should cease, you will regard such notice as a direction from the President to suspend them until further orders from this Department.' That is, I am required to respect the judgment of Mr. Trist, here, on passing events, purely *military*, as the judgment of the President, who is some two thousand miles off!

"I suppose this to be the second attempt of the kind ever made to dishonor a General-in-Chief in the field before or since the time of the French Convention. That other instance occurred in your absence from Washington in June, 1845, when Mr. Bancroft, Acting Secretary of War, instructed General Taylor in certain matters to obey the orders of Mr. Donaldson, *Chargé d'Affaires* in Texas; and you may remember the letter I wrote to General Taylor, with the permission of both Mr. Bancroft and yourself, to correct that blunder."

*　　*　　*　　*　　*　　*　　*　　*　　*

"Whenever it may please the President to instruct me directly, or through any authorized channel, to propose or to agree to an armistice with the enemy, on the happening of any given contingency, or to do any other military act, I shall most promptly and cheerfully obey him; but I entreat to be spared the personal dishonor of being again required to obey the orders of the chief clerk of the State Department."

*　　*　　*　　*　　*　　*　　*　　*　　*

"To Mr. Trist as a functionary of my Government, I have caused to be shown since his arrival here every proper attention. I sent the chief quartermaster and an aide-de-camp to show him the rooms I had ordered for him. I have caused him to be tendered a sentinel to be placed, etc. I shall, from time to time, send him word of my personal movements, and shall continue to show him all other attentions necessary to the discharge of any diplomatic function with which he may be entrusted."

The coolness between Mr. Trist and myself was much aggravated by accident. He fell ill at Vera Cruz, and was obliged to take much morphine to save life. Hence the offensive tone of certain letters. He several times relapsed. At Puebla, he was again dangerously ill, and I placed him under the special care of his and my friend, General Persifer F. Smith, at whose instance I visited his charge. My sympathy became deeply interested in his recovery, when he became my guest for more than six months. I never had a more amiable, quiet, or gentlemanly companion. He was highly respected by the Mexican authorities, and foreign diplomats residing in Mexico. The United

States could not have had a better representative. I am sorry to add that, poor and retaining all his good habits and talents, he has been strangely neglected by his Government up to this moment.

In occupying the capital and other cities, strict orders were given that no officer or man should be billeted, without consent, upon any inhabitant; that troops should only be quartered in the established barracks and such other public buildings as had been used for that purpose by the Mexican Government. Under this limitation, several large convents or monasteries, with but a few monks each, furnished ample quarters for many Americans, and, in every instance, the parties lived together in the most friendly manner, as was attested by the mutual tears shed by many, at the separation. Good order, or the protection of religion, persons, property, and industry were coextensive with the American rule. The highways, also, were comparatively freed from those old pests, robbers, or (the same thing) *rancheros*, who pillage, murder (often) all within their power, including their own priests. Everything consumed or used by our troops was as regularly paid for as if they had been at home. Hence Mexicans had never before known equal prosperity; for even the spirit of revolution, the chronic disease of the country, had been cured for the time.

Intelligent Mexicans, and, indeed, the great body of the people, felt and acknowledged the happy change. Hence, as soon as it was known that a treaty had been signed, political overtures from certain leaders were made to the General-in-Chief.

Of course, it was generally understood that, on the ratification of peace, about seven tenths of the whole rank and file of our regulars and all volunteers would stand, *ipso facto*, discharged from their enlistments, and also that all officers are always at liberty to resign their commissions after the execution of the last order. With the addition of ten or twenty *per centum* to the American pay, it would certainly have been easy to organize in Mexico an army of select American officers and men, say of fifteen thousand (to be kept up to that figure by recruits from home), to serve as a nucleus, which, with an equal native force, would suffice to hold the Republic in tranquillity and prosperity, under a new Government. The plan contemplated a *pronunciamento*, in which Scott should declare himself dictator of the Republic for a term of six or four years,—to give time to politicians and agitators to recover pacific habits, and to learn to govern themselves. Being already in possession of the principal forts, arsenals, founderies, mines, ports of entry and cities, with nearly all the arms of the country, it was not doubted that a very general acquiescence would soon have followed.

The plan was ultimately declined by Scott, though, to him, highly seductive both as to power and fortune, on two grounds: 1. It was required that he should pledge himself to slide, if possible, the Republic of Mexico into the Republic of the United States, which he deemed a measure, if successful, fraught with extreme peril to the free institutions of his country, and, 2. Because, although Scott had, in his official Report, No. 41 (December 25, 1847, page 560, above), suggested the question of annexation, President Polk's Government carefully withheld its wishes from him thereon.

The following sums of money came into the hands of the General-in-Chief in Mexico. About $12,000 captured at Cerro Gordo; $150,000 levied at the capital, in lieu of pillage; $50,000 (nearly) produced by the sale of captured Government tobacco, and two or three smaller sums for licenses, etc.,—making a total of about $220,000. The following disposition was made of this fund. A little more than $63,000 for extra blankets and shoes, distributed gratis among the rank and file; a considerable amount given to wounded men ($10 each) on leaving hospital; about $118,000 remitted to Washington to constitute a basis for an Army Asylum—for disabled men, not officers, and the remainder turned over, with the command, to Major-General Butler.

The treaty of peace was signed, February 2, 1848, and, in time, duly ratified at Washington, as I had in advance assured the Mexican authorities that it would be. On the 18th of the same month I received the President's instructions to turn over the command of the army in Mexico to Major-General William O. Butler (which I instantly did, in complimentary terms), and to submit myself to a court of inquiry—and such a court !—Towson, Cushing, and Belknap ! * —on its arrival at Mexico. The same mail brought orders restoring (from arrests) the three factious officers—Major-

---

* Brevet Brigadier-General Towson, president of the court, was duly brevetted a major-general, and Colonel Belknap brevetted a brigadier-general for their acceptable services in shielding Pillow and brow-beating Scott. The other member, General Cushing, in his pride as a lawyer and scholar, covered up his opinions in nice disquisitions and subtleties not always comprehended by his associates.

Generals Worth and Pillow, with Lieutenant-Colonel Duncan * — to their former commands and honors. Thus a series of the greatest wrongs ever heaped on a successful commander was consummated—in continuation of the Jackson persecution.

After a session of some weeks in Mexico, and some progress made in Pillow's case, the court was adjourned to meet next at Frederick, Maryland. Here the sessions were continued long enough to finish the whitewashing of Pillow by the means alluded to. The charges against Scott had been withdrawn under his open defiance of power and its minions, when the court was finally adjourned and dissolved.

* These three officers were not strictly confined to their respective quarters, as by law they must have been but for Scott's special indulgence in extending the limits of each, from the beginning of the arrest, to the city and its environs.

CHAPTER XXXVI.

ARRIVING at Vera Cruz, on my way home, I had a right to select the best steamer for my conveyance, and there were several at anchor off the castle in the service of the army. But the same reason that induced me to select non-effectives for oarsmen, the morning after the battle of Lundy's Lane, and, on the same occasion, to take a broken-down surgeon to attend me toward Philadelphia, now caused me to leave the steamers at Vera Cruz for the benefit of the corps soon to follow. Accordingly, I embarked in a small sailing brig, loaded down with guns, mortars, and ordnance stores.

25*

Sunday morning, May 20, we were, at daylight, boarded by the health officer at the Narrows, and I engaged a rowboat to take me to my family at Elizabeth. Having the Mexican disease upon me, I was in great want of repose and good nursing. I was, however, overpowered by deputations from New York; visited the city, and was honored with a most magnificent reception both civic and military.

At the instance of Scott, and in compliment to Taylor, then the regular nominee of the Whigs for the Presidency, Scott was limited to the command of the Eastern Department of the army, headquarters, New York; and the command of the Western Department was assigned to the other Major-General, Taylor, as in the time of the two Major-Generals, Brown and Jackson, in 1815, who commanded, down to 1821, the " *Divisions* " of the North and the South respectively.

Joint Resolution expressive of the Thanks of Congress to Major-General Winfield Scott, and the Troops under his command, for their distinguished Gallantry and good Conduct in the Campaign of eighteen hundred and forty-seven.

Resolved, unanimously, by the Senate and House of Representatives of the United States of America, in Congress assembled, That the thanks of Congress be, and they are hereby, presented to Winfield Scott, Major - General commanding in Chief the army in Mexico, and through him, to the officers and men of the regular and volunteer corps under him, for their uniform gallantry and good conduct, conspicuously displayed at the siege and capture of the City of Vera Cruz and castle of San Juan de Ulloa, March twenty-ninth, eighteen hundred and forty-seven; and in the successive battles of Cerro Gordo, April eighteenth; Contreras, San Antonio, and Churubusco, August nineteenth and twentieth; and for the victories achieved in front of the City of Mexico, September eighth, eleventh, twelfth, and thirteenth, and the capture of the metropolis, September fourteenth, eighteen hundred and forty-seven, in which the Mexican troops, greatly superior in numbers, and with every advantage of position, were in every conflict signally defeated by the American arms.

Sec. 2. *Resolved*, That the President of the United States be, and he is hereby, requested to cause to be struck a gold medal, with devices emblematical of the series of brilliant victories achieved by the army, and presented to Major-General Winfield Scott, as a testimony of the high sense entertained by Congress of his valor, skill, and judicious conduct in the memorable campaign of eighteen hundred and forty-seven.

Sec. 3. *Resolved*, That the President of the United States be requested to cause the foregoing resolutions to be communicated to Major-General Scott, in such terms as he may deem best calculated to give effect to the objects thereof.

Approved, *March* 9, 1848.

It was enacted in 1798, that a lieutenant-general should be appointed, and General Washington accepted the office.   The next year the grade of full general was provided for, and the law declared that on filling the latter, the former should stand repealed.   On the next meeting of Congress, President Adams being a little dilatory in nominating to the new place, the Father of his country died a lieutenant-general, and, consequently, the act providing for that appointment was never repealed.

IN SENATE.

February 24, 1849, Hon. Mr. Fitzgerald " asked and obtained leave to bring in a joint resolution to confer upon Major-General Winfield Scott the brevet rank of lieutenant-general, which was read and passed to a second reading." •

A motion to read the resolution a third time the same day being objected to by a single Senator, the subject went over for the want of time, Congress being within a week of dissolution.

July 29, 1850, Hon. Mr. Clemens submitted the following:

" *Resolved*, That the Committee on Military Affairs be instructed to inquire into the expediency of conferring by law the brevet rank of lieutenant-general on Major-General Winfield Scott, with such additional pay and allowances as may be deemed proper, in consideration of the distinguished services rendered to the Republic by that officer during the late war with Mexico."

Eight days later that resolution was referred to the Senate's Military Committee.

On the last day of the session (September 30, 1850), Hon. Jefferson Davis, Chairman, reported the following resolution on the same subject:

" *Resolved*, That the President of the United States be, and he is hereby, requested to refer to an army board of officers, to be designated by him, the following questions, viz. :

" Is it expedient or necessary to provide for additional grades of commissioned officers in the army of the United States; and, if so, what grades, in addition to the present organization, should be created ? "

This was an ingenious fetch of Mr. Davis, not doubting that jealousies in the service would give a quietus to the lieutenant-generalcy ; but when the report came in, though in reply to his own call, he dropped it as repugnant to his cherished hatred. See original ground of his hostility, page 198 (note), above. Mr. Davis, moreover, was the heir to his father-in-law's prejudices (—General Taylor's), who, for a long time, spurned him.

In pursuance of this request, the President of the United States appointed a board of officers—Generals Jesup (President), Wool, Gibson, Totten, Talcott, Hitchcock, and Colonel Crane—who reported *unanimously,* as follows :

" Under the first inquiry referred to it, the Board is of opinion that it is expedient to create by law for the army the additional grade of lieutenant-general, and that when, in the opinion of the President and

Senate, it shall be deemed proper to acknowledge eminent services of officers of the army, and in the mode
already provided for in subordinate grades, it is expedient and proper that the grade of lieutenant-general
may be conferred by brevet."

December 17, 1850, that report was laid before
the Senate, and referred to the Committee on Military
Affairs, etc.

January 25, 1851, Hon. Mr. Shields reported a
joint resolution in conformity with the recommendation
of the Military Board.

February 13, 1851, the joint resolution passed the
Senate by 31 votes to 16, several of its friends (among
them the Hon. Mr. Clemens) being absent.

HOUSE OF REPRESENTATIVES.

March 3, 1851, an attempt was made by the Hon.
A. H. Stephens to call up, out of turn, the joint reso-
lution (about the ninetieth of the bills, etc., on the
Speaker's table), when the yeas were 112, to 72 nays;
several of the friends of the measure—among them the
Hon. Mr. Gorman—happening to be out of their seats.
The same motion was repeated the same evening, by
the Hon. Mr. Toombs, with a like result. A change

of some eight or ten votes would have made a two-thirds majority.

IN SENATE.

December 8, 1851, Hon. Mr. Clemens asked and obtained leave to bring in a joint resolution, " authorizing the President of the United States to confer the title of lieutenant-general by brevet for eminent services; which was read the first and second time, by unanimous consent, and referred to the Committee on Military Affairs." (This joint resolution is similar to the one on the same subject passed by the Senate at the preceding session.)

December 23, 1851, the joint resolution was reported back to the Senate without amendment, and slept the remainder of the session.

December 7, 1852, (the second day of the new session,) Hon. Mr. Clemens again brought up the same resolution in the Senate, and it passed that body on the 21st, by a vote of 34 to 12.

The resolution having been again passed by the Senate was taken up in the House by the resolute Judge Bailey, and passed through all the forms of legislation before resuming his seat.

Mr. Jefferson Davis, soon in the Cabinet, allowed of no intermission in his hostility. The rank could not be withheld; but he next resolved it should carry no additional compensation, however clearly embraced. Yet he permitted the question of compensation to go to the Attorney-General; but coupled the reference with a volunteer argument of fourteen pages — against the claim — he, himself, being profoundly ignorant of law—for the benefit of the law-officer of the Government! It is true he informed me that he had made the reference; but I was purely indebted to accident for my knowledge of his *legal* argument.

To overcome this deadly enemy, my friends in the two Houses of Congress, including quite a roll of Democrats, had again to push through all the forms of legislation a *declaratory* provision that gave me what might reasonably be claimed under the first enactment. I regret being unable to insert all the names of these noble Democrats; but Shields led in the Senate, and Clingham in the House, most triumphantly.

But I was not even yet out of the hands of Mr. Davis. The declaratory resolution standing alone, he would certainly have caused it to be vetoed. The danger was perceived by all my friends, and their next step was to embody it in the Military Appropriation Bill. Another triumph. It was the last hour of the administration. The President and his whole Cabinet were, as is usual, in a drawing-room adjoining the Senate chamber, and the Secretaries much on the floor of the latter. My friends appointed several of their number to keep an eye on the engrossing clerk, lest, in copying a great number of amendments, he might not *accidentally* leave out my resolution. And thus it might be said (with due extravagance) of another old soldier—

"Thrice he routed all his foes and thrice he slew the slain."

On the inauguration of President Taylor, Scott, though again assuming the command of the whole army, continued his headquarters at New York, not being called to Washington on account of the personal hostility of the President; but on the succession of President Fillmore (in 1850) the headquarters of the General-in-Chief were reëstablished at Washington, and there continued till the accession of President Pierce, when by request of Scott, there was another change back to New York. Here his office remained down to his retirement from command, in 1861, though his last ten months on duty—hard, disabling service—were spent in Washington.

Among the incidents of this period, the autobiographer's third and greatest humiliation in politics must not be omitted. The first (but slight) happened in the Whig Convention at Harrisburg, in 1839; the second at the Philadelphia Convention in 1848, that nominated Taylor. (Certain Whigs—several still living—may thank me that I do not here expose their vile tricks on that occasion; but I have long forgiven them.)

In June, 1852, the Whig Convention that met at Baltimore, to choose candidates to be run in the following November, for President and Vice-President, after a great number of ballots finally put the autobiographer in nomination for the Presidency. His competitors, before that body, were the actual President, Mr. Fillmore, and Mr. Webster, Secretary of State. William A. Graham, the Secretary of the Navy, was chosen as the candidate for the Vice-Presidency on the same ticket, and General Pierce had, some time before, been made the Democratic candidate for the higher office.

It is very generally held that the leaders of a party are bound to support its regular nominations, particularly such leaders as sought the honor of nomination by the body appointed to select candidates. Mr. Fillmore, who was ambitious of another executive term, disregarded this obligation. He, with several of his Cabinet, in a huff, openly eschewed the nomination. Mr. Webster, already *moribond* (he died before the election), acted on the occasion as if he had been cheated out of a rightful inheritance, and stimulated his son and several leading friends to take an active part on the side of his resentment. He failed, however, to influence the vote of his noble State.

At the election, Scott was signally defeated—receiving only the votes of Massachusetts, Vermont, Kentucky, and Tennessee. Virginia, his dear mother State, utterly repudiated him—her wiseacres preferring a succession or two more of pliant administrations to pave the way for rebellion and ruin.

The mortification of the defeated candidate was, however, nearly lost in the following reflections:

1. In the nomination and election of high functionaries, since the days of " modern degeneracy " (*Jacksonism*), the virtue and wisdom of candidates have had but

little if any weight, either in primary movements or at the polls. It would, therefore, be illogical to ascribe Scott's defeat in the election of 1852, exclusively to his demerits—positive or comparative.

2. Scott was a Whig. The conflicts, however, between Mr. Clay and President Tyler, combined with the ambiguous position of Mr. Webster ("Where am I to go?"), had pretty well run the party. *under ground;* for Taylor, though nominated on the same basis, and throwing out in the canvass side glances at the other party, was, nevertheless, a minority President. The outsiders—Whig office-seekers—it is true, worked like beavers for him; but the split in the Democratic ranks —running two candidates—Cass and Van Buren—decided the election.

3. In 1852, Scott had not one of those adventitious helps. The Democrats were thoroughly united. Their famished office-*seekers*, remembering their long enjoyment of the flesh-pots of Government, were desperately bent on the recovery of their old livings; whereas, now there was nothing left for the outsiders, the universal Whig office-*holders*, "a careless herd, full of the pasture," — "fat and greasy citizens" — were happy to follow the example of Mr. Fillmore and abstain from

any interference in the election—in accordance, also, with the known principles and wishes of Scott. Hence the issue went against him as if *by default.*

For his political defeats, the autobiographer cannot too often return thanks to God. As he has said before, they proved benefits to him. Have they been such to his country? This is a point that may, perhaps, hereafter be doubted by calm inquirers.

The following extracts present a subject that needs no explanation :

" *Kansas and Scott.*

" Mr. Crittenden's resolution, in relation to sending General Scott to Kansas, to take command of the United States troops there, was taken up in the Senate, yesterday, and warmly discussed. The resolution was ably advocated by Senators Crittenden, Bell, Clayton, and Seward, and opposed by Messrs. Brown, of Mississippi, Toucey, Mallory, and Mason. The Senate adjourned without any decision on the subject. The proposition to send General Scott to Kansas, with power to settle the difficulties existing there according to his own judgment, appears to have occurred to several persons simultaneously. It was suggested by the Albany *Evening Journal;* and Hon. Robert C. Winthrop, in a letter written early last week, in reference to the Kansas meeting in Faneuil Hall, says:

"'I cannot help thinking that, if the gallant veteran, who ought at this moment to have been at the head of the nation, and who is still at the head of its army—whose presence has almost as often been the pledge of peace, in scenes of strife, as it has been of victory on the field of battle—could be sent at once to Kansas, with full powers to command and enforce a cessation of lawless violence and conflict, and to put down the reign of terror in that region, the dangers which now threaten the peace of the whole country might still be averted.'

"But the administration Senators profess to believe that the Kansas difficulty is 'not much of a shower,' and the only thing they recommend is to stop agitating the matter, when the difficulties will settle themselves of their own accord. But the greatest difficulty of all they will find will be to stop the agitation. It must be agitated until the cause of the agitation shall have been removed."—*New York Times*, June 12, 1856.

"If General Scott could be sent to Kansas with instructions to restore and maintain peace and order, and with a liberal discretion as to the means to be employed to effect that object, we should feel a moral certainty of his triumphant and glorious success. But to send him there to obey the instructions of Jeff. Davis and enforce the acts of the tyrannical bogus Legislature would be to lacerate his feelings, tarnish his proud fame, and probably hasten his descent to the tomb. As the mere instrument of Davis and Shannon, Marshal Donaldson, and 'Sheriff' Jones, we do not see how he could do better than Colonel Sumner has done, while the employment would be entirely beneath his position and alien to his character. If such be the work contemplated, we trust a fitter instrument will be selected."—*New York Tribune*, June 12, 1856.

During the thirteen years following the peace with Mexico, but few incidents of historical interest to the autobiographer occurred.

As belonging to the history of the times, the subjoined letter may be here inserted.

On the occasion of a threatened renewal of pol'tical agitations in the Canadas, the autobiographer being interrogated on the subject by an eminent citizen and a friend, replied:

To John C. Hamilton, Esquire.

WEST POINT, *June* 29, 1849.

MY DEAR SIR:

The news from the Parliament of Great Britain this morning must, I think, increase the discontents of our neighbors on the other side of the St. Lawrence and the lakes not a little; and that those discontents may in a few years lead to a separation of the Canadas, New Brunswick, etc., etc., from England seems equally probable.

Will those Provinces form themselves into an independent nation, or seek a connection with our Union? I think the probability is greatly in favor of the latter. In my judgment the interests of both sides would be much promoted by annexation—the several Provinces coming into the Union on equal terms with our present thirty States. The free navigation of the St. Lawrence is already of immense importance to, perhaps, a third of our present population, and would be of great value to the remainder.

26

After annexation, two revenue cutters below Quebec would give us a better security against smuggling than thirty thousand custom - house *employés* strung along the line that separates us from the British possessions on our continent. I am well acquainted with that line, and know a great deal about the interests and character of the Provincials. Though opposed to incorporating with us any district densely peopled with the *Mexican* race, I should be most happy to fraternize with our northern and northeastern neighbors.

What may be the views of our Executive Government on the subject, I know absolutely nothing; but I think I cannot err in saying that two thirds of our people would rejoice at the incorporation, and the other third soon perceive its benefits.

Of course I am opposed to any underhanded measures on our part, in favor of the measure, or any other act of bad faith toward Great Britain. Her good will, in my view of the matter, is only second to that of the Provincials themselves, and that the former would soon follow the latter—considering the present temper and condition of Christendom—cannot be doubted.

The foregoing views I have long been in the habit

of expressing in conversation. I give them to you for what they may be worth.

Faithfully yours,

WINFIELD SCOTT.

J. C. HAMILTON, ESQ.

Mr. Hamilton, a pious son—a large contributor to our early history—in the Life and Times of his father,* and also as the editor of a recent and most accurate edition of the *Federalist*—with a splendid introduction and valuable notes—has had the kindness to refer the autobiographer to the following interesting facts in regard to the Canadas.

In the Articles of Confederation (the 11th) it was provided: " Canada acceding to this Confederation, and joining in the measures of the United States, shall be admitted into and entitled to all the advantages of this Union; but no other colony shall be admitted into the same, unless such admission be agreed to by *nine* States."

Several attempts were made to bring those Prov-

---

* The exact title of this able work is—*History of the Republic of the United States, as traced in the Writings of Alexander Hamilton and of his Contemporaries*, 7 vols. 8vo.

inces (Upper and Lower Canada) into the Union, down to 1797; but from various causes they failed, though a favorite object with a large portion of the Union.

The expedition set on foot by Mr. Secretary Floyd, in 1857, against the Mormons and Indians about Salt Lake was, beyond a doubt, to give occasion for large contracts and expenditures, that is, to open a wide field for frauds and peculation. This purpose was not comprehended nor scarcely suspected in, perhaps, a year; but, observing the desperate characters who frequented the Secretary, some of whom had desks near him, suspicion was at length excited. Scott protested against the expedition on the general ground of inexpediency, and specially because the season was too late for the troops to reach their destination in comfort or even in safety. Particular facts, observed by different officers, if united, would prove the imputation. The Governor of the Territory, Mr. Cumming; the commander of the troops, Brigadier-General A. S. Johnston, and our officers, stood above all suspicion of complicity.

An incident occurred in 1859 on the Pacific coast which the President regarded as endangering not a little our peaceful relations with Great Britain. At the moment when commissioners were engaged in running the boundary line between the two countries, but differing as to which party the San Juan Island, in Puget's Sound, should be assigned, the question of course reverted to the two paramount Governments. Brigadier-General Harney, who commanded our forces in that quarter, was a great favorite with the five Democratic Presidents. Full of blind admiration for his patrons, he had before, in Florida, hung several Indians, under the most doubtful circumstances, in imitation of a like act on the part of General Jackson, in the same quarter, and now, as that popular hero gained much applause by wrenching Pensacola and all Middle Florida from Spain, in time of peace, Harney probably thought he might make himself President too, by cutting short all diplomacy and taking forcible possession of the disputed island! Imitations on the part of certain people always begin by copying defects. President Buchanan, however, well knowing the difference in power between Spain and Great Britain, kindly inquired of the autobiographer (now recently a cripple from a fall) whether, without injury, he could go on a mission to Puget's Sound? The voyage, *via* Panama, was promptly undertaken, and Scott sailed from New York, September 20, 1859, in *The Star of the West.*

Arriving in the Sound, near the British Governor at Victoria, a few courteous notes restored the island to its late neutral condition—the joint possession of the two parties. It is not known that the *protegé*, Harney, was even reprimanded for his rashness. He certainly was not recalled, although the measure was suggested by the writer.

Perhaps but few readers will complain of the insertion, in this narrative, of the following poem, written by Mrs. Scott, then in Paris, to cheer her husband on in his mission of peace. An English lady, a friend of the authoress, begged permission to copy the poem, which she sent to the London *Ladies' Magazine.*

> Oh, Star of the West! throw thy radiance benign,
>   Unchanging and strong, on the warrior's way!
> May the waves that surround him, by favor divine,
>   Be as lustrous and calm as thine own cheering ray.
>
> " The hero of many a battle " goes now
>   More joyfully forth on a mission of peace:
> Oh! Star of the West! be the prototype thou
>   Of success, whose pure blessings shall never surcease.
>
> God prosper the barque that hath borrowed thy name!
>   Supplications, heartborn, to his throne are address'd
> For the good, and the brave, and the pious, who claim
>   Our devotion—our prayers—in the " Star of the West."

They go, all unarm'd—save, with holiest views—
  The ills of ambition and strife to arrest;
And the spirit of St. John (loved Apostle) imbues
  Hearts, approaching his Isle, in the "Star of the West."

Unarm'd they will land! 'mid contention and wrath;
  But, on high, 'tis decreed that "Peacemakers be blest."
They will follow, once more, their long, long ocean path,
  And regain their own shores, with the "Star of the West."

Sail on, gallant Scott! true disciple of virtue!
  Whose justice and faith every danger will breast
Nor swerve in the conflict. Heaven will not desert you,
  There are angels on guard 'round the "Star of the West."

PARIS, *October* 6, 1859.

Of my many persevering efforts to improve the
condition of the army, and, consequently, its efficiency,
several proofs have been embodied in this narrative.
The General Order reproduced at page 361, had in
view, mainly, the protection of the rank and file
against the abuses of commissioned and non-commissioned officers. I shall here add two other measures
which greatly improved the comforts and usefulness of
commissioned officers generally. 1. I claim credit for
a long and active correspondence with military committees in the two Houses of Congress, resulting in the
law that has given, since 1834, the cumulative rations

to our medical officers, that has prevented many of the most valuable from resigning on obtaining high professional skill by experience.   2. And I claim also a special agency in procuring the provision giving, since 1838, to " every commissioned officer of the line or staff, *exclusive of general officers*," " one additional ration per diem, for every five years he may have served, or shall serve, in the army of the United States."   For several years in succession I had written and pressed upon the two military committees of Congress a section to that effect.   Passing through Washington to the Cherokee country, in 1838, the Hon. Gouverneur Kemble, an intelligent friend of the army and member of the House Committee, called upon me on the part of the body to say that, although they could report the bill, and might carry it in the House against all opposition; yet if the chairman of the committee (McKay) and another radical member (Walter Coles) should speak against the measure in the House, its passage would be doubtful.   Hence the desire that I should meet the committee.

I found the chairman gruff and immovable.   At length he grumbled out — " Have you not pay enough ? "   I rejoined: " Leave me out; leave out the generals." He added, " Agreed," and thence the service ration.

By that suggestion, it may be that I have lost, up to the present time (twenty-six years), the current receipts from five hundred to a thousand dollars a year, which would have been a great comfort to the declining years of an old soldier, as the bill might, in a year or two more, if not in 1838, have been passed—nothing being more reasonable—without excluding the general officers.

But an increase of physical infirmities admonishes me to bring this narrative to a close. Happily but little remains to be added.

In the Presidential canvass of 1860, it was plainly seen that a disruption of the Union was imminent. Deeply impressed with the danger, I addressed a memorial to President Buchanan on the subject, of which the following are extracts :

" October 29, 1860.

" The excitement that threatens secession is caused by the near prospect of a Republican's election to the Presidency. From a sense of propriety, as a soldier, I have taken no part in the pending canvass, and, as always heretofore, mean to stay away from the polls.

26*

My sympathies, however, are with the Bell and Everett ticket. With Mr. Lincoln I have had no communication whatever, direct or indirect, and have no recollection of ever having seen his person; but cannot believe any unconstitutional violence or breach of law, is to be apprehended from his administration of the Federal Government.

"From a knowledge of our Southern population it is my solemn conviction that there is some danger of an early act of rashness preliminary to secession, viz., the seizure of some or all of the following posts : Forts Jackson and St. Philip, on the Mississippi, below New Orleans, both without garrisons; Fort Morgan, below Mobile, without a garrison; Forts Pickens and McKee, Pensacola Harbor, with an insufficient garrison for one; Fort Pulaski, below Savannah, without a garrison; Forts Moultrie and Sumter, Charleston Harbor, the former with an insufficient garrison, and the latter without any; and Fort Monroe, Hampton Roads, without a sufficient garrison. In my opinion all these works should be immediately so garrisoned as to make any attempt to take any one of them, by surprise or *coup de main*, ridiculous.

"With the army faithful to its allegiance, and the

navy probably equally so, and with a Federal Executive, for the next twelve months, of firmness and moderation, which the country has a right to expect—*moderation* being an element of power not less than *firmness*—there is good reason to hope that the danger of secession may be made to pass away without one conflict of arms, one execution, or one arrest for treason. In the mean time it is suggested that exports might be left perfectly free—and to avoid conflicts all duties on imports be collected outside of the cities, in forts or ships of war."

The inauguration of President Lincoln was, perhaps, the most critical and hazardous event with which I have ever been connected. In the preceding two months I had received more than fifty letters, many from points distant from each other—some earnestly dissuading me from being present at the event, and others distinctly threatening assassination if I dared to protect the ceremony by a military force. The election having been entirely regular, I resolved that the Constitution should not be overturned by violence if I could possibly prevent it. Accordingly, I caused to be organized the *élite* of the Washington Volunteers, and called from a distance two batteries of horse artillery, with small detachments of cavalry and infantry, all regulars.

In concert with Congressional Committees of arrangements, the President was escorted to and from the Capitol by volunteers—the regulars, with whom I marched, flanking the movement in parallel streets,—only I claimed the place immediately in front of the President for the fine company of Sappers and Miners under Captain Duane of the Engineers. To this choice body of men it was only necessary to say : *The honor of our country is in your hands.*

With a view to freedom of movement, I remained just outside of the Capitol Square with the light batteries. The procession returned to the President's mansion in the same order, and happily the Government was saved.

To show the new Administration that it was from no neglect of mine that several of our Southern forts had fallen into the hands of the rebels, I drew up and submitted the following defensive statement in March, 1861 :

Southern Forts.

October 29, 1860.—I emphatically, as has been seen, called the attention of the President to the necessity of strong garrisons in all the forts below the principal commercial cities of the Southern States, including, by name, the forts in Pensacola Harbor, etc.

October 31.—I suggested to the Secretary of War that a circular should be sent at once to such of those forts as had garrisons, to be on the alert against surprises and sudden assaults.*

After a long confinement to my bed, in New York, I came to this city (Washington), December 12. Next day I personally urged upon the Secretary of War the same views, viz.: strong garrisons in the Southern forts—those of Charleston and Pensacola Harbors, at once; those on Mobile Bay and the Mississippi, below New Orleans, next, etc., etc. I again pointed out the organized companies and the recruits at the principal dépôts available for the purpose. The Secretary did not concur in one of my views, when I begged him to procure for me an early interview with the President,

* Permission not granted.

that I might make one effort more to save the forts and the Union.

By appointment, the Secretary accompanied me to the President, December 15, when the same topics, secessionism, etc., were again pretty fully discussed. There being, at the moment, in the opinion of the President, no danger of an early secession, beyond South Carolina, the President, in reply to my arguments for immediately reënforcing Fort Moultrie, and sending a garrison to Fort Sumter, said, in substance, the time had not arrived for doing so; that he would wait the action of the Convention of South Carolina, in the expectation that a commission would be appointed and sent to negotiate with him and Congress, respecting the secession of the State and the property of the United States held within its limits; and that, if Congress should decide against the secession, then he would send a reënforcement, and telegraph the commanding officer (Major Anderson) of Fort Moultrie, to hold the forts (Moultrie and Sumter) against attack.

And the Secretary, with animation, added: "We have a vessel of war (the Brooklyn) held in readiness at Norfolk, and he would then send three hundred men, in her, from Fort Monroe, to Charleston." To which I replied, first, "That so many men could not be withdrawn from that garrison, but could be taken from New York. Next, that it would then be too late, as the South Carolina Commissioners would have the game in their hands—by first using, and then cutting the wires; that, as there was not a soldier in Fort Sumter, any handful of armed secessionists might seize and occupy it," etc., etc.

Here the remark may be permitted, that, if the Secretary's three hundred men had then (or some time later) been sent to Forts Moultrie and Sumter, *both* would now have been in the possession of the United States, and not a battery, below them, could have been erected by the Secessionists. Consequently, the access to those forts from the sea would now (the end of March, 1861) be unobstructed and *free.*

"The plan invented by General Scott to stop secession was, like all campaigns devised by him, very able in its details and nearly certain of general success. The Southern States are full of arsenals and forts, commanding their rivers and strategic points. General Scott desired to transfer the army of the United States to these forts as speedily and as quietly as possible.

The Southern States could not cut off communication between the Government and the fortresses without a great fleet, which they cannot build for years—or take them by land without one hundred thousand men, many hundred millions of dollars, several campaigns, and many a bloody siege. Had Scott been able to have got these forts in the condition he desired them to be, the Southern Confederacy would not now exist." —*Part of the Eulogy pronounced on Secretary Floyd, by the Richmond Examiner, on his reception at that city.*

The same day, December 15, I wrote the following note:

"Lieutenant-General Scott begs the President to pardon him for supplying, in this note, what he omitted to say this morning, at the interview with which he was honored by the President. 1. Long *prior* to the *Force Bill* (March 2, 1833), prior to the issue of his proclamation, and, in part, *prior* to the passage of the ordinance of nullification—President Jackson, under the act of March 3, 1807—'authorizing the employment of the land and naval forces'—caused reënforcements to be sent to Fort Moultrie, and a sloop-of-war (the Natchez), with two revenue cutters, to be sent to Charleston Harbor [all under Scott], in order to prevent the seizure of that fort by the nullifiers, and 2. To insure the execution of the revenue laws—General Scott himself arrived at Charleston the day after the passage of the ordinance of nullification, and many of the additional companies were then in route for the same destination.

"President Jackson familiarly said at the time: 'That, by the assemblage of those forces, for lawful purposes, he was not making war upon South Carolina; but that if South Carolina attacked them, it would be South Carolina that made war upon the United States.'

"General Scott, who received his first instructions (oral) from the President, Jackson, in the temporary absence of the Secretary of War (General Cass), remembers those expressions well.

"*Saturday night, December* 15, 1860."

December 28.—Again, after Major Anderson had gallantly and wisely thrown his handful of men from Fort Moultrie into Fort Sumter—learning that, on demand of South Carolina, there was great danger he might be. ordered by the Secretary back to the less tenable work, or *out* of the harbor, I wrote this note to the Secretary of War:

"Lieutenant-General Scott (who has had a bad night, and can scarcely hold up his head this morning) begs to express the hope to the Secretary of War—1. That orders may not be given for the evacuation of Fort Sumter; 2. That one hundred and fifty recruits may instantly be sent from Governor's Island to reënforce that garrison, with ample supplies of ammunition and subsistence, including fresh vegetables, as potatoes, onions, turnips, etc; 3. That one or two armed vessels be sent to support the said fort.

"Lieutenant-General Scott avails himself of this opportunity also to express the hope that the recommendation heretofore made by him to the Secretary of War, respecting Forts Jackson, St. Philip, Morgan, and Pulaski, and particularly in respect to Forts Pickens and McRee, and the Pensacola Navy Yard, in connection with the last two named works, may be reconsidered by the Secretary.

"Lieutenant-General Scott will further ask the attention of the Secretary to Forts Jefferson (Tortugas), and Taylor (Key West), which are wholly national—being of far greater value even to the most distant points of the Atlantic Coast and the people on the upper waters of the Missouri, Mississippi, and Ohio Rivers, than to the State of Florida. There is only a feeble company at Key West for the defence of Fort Taylor, and not a soldier in Fort Jefferson to resist a handful of fillibusters or a rowboat of pirates; and the Gulf, soon after the beginning of secession or revolutionary troubles in the adjacent States, will swarm with such nuisances."

December 30.—I addressed the President again, as follows:

"Lieutenant-General Scott begs the President of the United States to pardon the irregularity of this communication. It is Sunday, the weather is bad, and General Scott is not well enough even to go to church.

"But matters of the highest national importance seem to forbid a moment's delay, and, if misled by zeal, he hopes for the President's forgiveness.

"Will the President permit General Scott, without reference to the War Department,* and, otherwise, as

---

* The Secretary was already suspected.

secretly as possible, to send two hundred and fifty re-cruits, from New York Harbor, to reënforce Fort Sumter, together with some extra muskets or rifles, ammunition, and subsistence.

"It is hoped that a sloop-of-war and cutter may be ordered, for the same purpose, as early as to-morrow.

"General Scott will wait upon the President at any moment he may be called for."

The South Carolina Commissioners had already been many days in Washington, and no movement of defence (on the part of the United States) was per-mitted.

I will here close my notice of Fort Sumter by quoting from some of my previous reports.

It would have been easy to reënforce this fort down to about the 12th of February. In this long delay Fort Moultrie had been rearmed and greatly strengthened, in every way, by the rebels. Many powerful new land batteries (besides a formidable raft) had been constructed. Hulks, too, were sunk in the principal channel, so as to render access to Fort Sumter from the sea impracticable, without first carrying all the lower batteries of the Secessionists. The difficulty of reënforcing had thus been increased ten or twelve fold. First, the late

President refused to allow any attempt to be made, because he was holding negotiations with the South Carolina Commissioners ; afterward, Secretary Holt and myself endeavored, in vain, to obtain a ship of war for the purpose, and were finally obliged to employ the passenger steamer the *Star of the West.* That vessel, but for the hesitation of the master, might, as is generally believed, have delivered at the fort the men and subsistence on board. This attempt at succor failing, I next verbally submitted to the late Cabinet, either that succor be sent by ships of war, fighting their way by the batteries (increasing in strength daily), or that Major Anderson should be left to ameliorate his condition by the muzzles of his guns; that is, enforcing supplies by bombardment, and by *bringing to* merchant vessels, helping himself (giving orders for payment), or, finally, be allowed to evacuate the fort, which, in that case, would be inevitable.

But before any resolution was taken—the late Secretary of the Navy making difficulties about the want of suitable war vessels — another Commissioner from South Carolina arrived, causing further delay. When this had passed away, Secretaries Holt and Toucey, Captain Ward of the Navy and myself—with the knowledge of the President (Buchanan)—settled upon the employment, under the Captain (who was eager for the expedition), of three or four small steamers, belonging to the Coast Survey. At that time (late in January), I have but little doubt, Captain Ward would have reached Fort Sumter, with all his vessels. But he was kept back by something like a *truce* or armistice made (here), embracing Charleston and Pensacola Harbors, agreed upon between the late President and certain principal seceders of South Carolina, Florida, Louisiana, etc., and this truce lasted to the end of that administration.

* * * * * * * * *

It was not till January 3 (when the first Commissioners from South Carolina withdrew) that the permission I had solicited, October 31, was obtained—to admonish commanders of the few Southern forts (with garrisons) to be on the alert against surprises and sudden assaults. (Major Anderson was not among the admonished, being already straitly beleaguered.)

January 3.—To Lieutenant Slemmer, Commanding in Pensacola Harbor:

"The General-in-Chief directs that you take measures to do the utmost in your power to prevent the seizure of either of the forts in Pensacola Harbor, by surprise or assault—consulting first with the Commander of the Navy Yard, who will, probably, have received instructions to coöperate with you." (This order was signed by Aide-de-Camp Lay.).

It was just before the surrender of the Pensacola Navy Yard (January 12) that Lieutenant Slemmer, calling upon Commodore Armstrong, obtained the aid of some thirty common seamen or laborers (but no marines), which, added to his forty-six soldiers, made up his numbers to seventy-six men, with whom this meritorious officer has since held Fort Pickens, and performed (working night and day) an immense amount of labor in mounting guns, keeping up a strong guard, etc., etc.

Early in January I renewed (as has been seen) my solicitations to be allowed to reënforce Fort Pickens; but a good deal of time was lost in vacillations. First, the President "thought, if no movement is made by the United States, Fort McRee will probably not be occupied, nor Fort Pickens attacked. In case of movement by the United States, which will doubtless be made known by the wires, there will be corresponding local movements, and the attempt to reënforce will be useless." (Quotation from a note made by Aide-de-Camp Lay, about January 12, of the President's reply to a message from me.) Next, it was doubted whether it would be safe to send reënforcements in an unarmed steamer, and the want, *as usual*, of a suitable naval vessel—the Brooklyn being long held in reserve at Norfolk for some purpose unknown to me. Finally, after I had kept a body of three hundred recruits in New York Harbor ready for some time — (and they would have been sufficient to reënforce, temporarily, Fort Pickens, and to occupy Fort McRee also) — the President, about January 18, directed that the sloop-of-war Brooklyn should take a single company (ninety men from Fort Monroe, Hampton Roads), and reenforce Lieutenant Slemmer, in Fort Pickens, but without a surplus man for the neighboring fort, McRee !

The Brooklyn, with Captain Vogdes' Company alone, left the Chesapeake, for Fort Pickens, about January 22, and on the 29th, President Buchanan, having entered into a *quasi* armistice with certain leading seceders at Pensacola and elsewhere, caused Secretaries Holt and Toucey to instruct, in a joint note, the commanders of the war vessels off Pensacola and Lieutenant Slemmer, commanding Fort Pickens, to commit no act of hostility, and not to land Captain Vogdes' Company unless that fort should be attacked!

*   *   *   *   *   *   *   *   *

It was known at the Navy Department that the Brooklyn, with Captain Vogdes on board, would be obliged in open sea to stand off and on Fort Pickens, and, in rough weather, might sometimes be fifty miles off. Indeed, if so at sea, the fort might have been attacked and easily carried before the reënforcement could have reached the beach (in open sea), where alone it could land.

Respectfully submitted,

WINFIELD SCOTT.

HEADQUARTERS OF THE ARMY, ⎱
  WASHINGTON, *March* 30, 1861. ⎰

WASHINGTON, *March* 3, 1861.

DEAR SIR:

Hoping that in a day or two the new President will have happily passed through all personal danger,

27

and find himself installed an honored successor of the great Washington, with you as the chief of his Cabinet —I beg leave to repeat in writing what I have before said to you orally — this Supplement to my printed " Views " (dated in October last) on the highly disordered condition of our (so late) happy and glorious Union.

To meet the extraordinary exigencies of the times, it seems to me that I am guilty of no arrogance in limiting the President's field of selection to one of the four plans of procedure subjoined:

I. Throw off the *old* and assume a *new* designation —the *Union Party;* adopt the conciliatory measures proposed by Mr. Crittenden or the Peace Convention, and, my life upon it, we shall have no new case of Secession; but on the contrary, an early return of many, if not of all the States which have already broken off from the Union. Without some equally benign measure, the remaining slaveholding States will probably join the Montgomery Confederacy in less than sixty days—when this city, being included in a foreign country, would require a permanent garrison of at least thirty-five thousand troops, to protect the Government within it.

II. Collect the duties on foreign goods *outside* the ports of which this Government has lost the command, or close such ports by act of Congress, and blockade them.

III. Conquer the seceded States by invading armies. No doubt this might be done in two or three years, by a young and able general—a Wolfe—a Desaix, or a Hoche, with three hundred thousand disciplined men [kept up to that number], estimating a third for garrisons, and the loss of a yet greater number by skirmishes, sieges, battles, and Southern fevers. The destruction of life and property on the other side would be frightful—however perfect the moral discipline of the invaders. The conquest completed, at that enormous waste of human life to the North and Northwest, with at least $250,000,000 added thereto, and *Cui bono?* Fifteen devastated Provinces! not to be brought into harmony with their conquerors; but to be held for generations by heavy garrisons, at an expense quadruple the net duties or taxes which it would be possible to extort from them, followed by a Protector or an Emperor.

IV. Say to the seceded States— *Wayward Sisters, depart in peace !*

In haste, I remain,

Very truly yours,

WINFIELD SCOTT.

Hon. William H. Seward.

But few contemporaries have been more highly complimented with literary distinctions and testimonials of public esteem than the autobiographer. A designation of some of those precious muniments he cannot deny himself the pleasure of citing in this narrative:

Nassau Hall, Princeton, conferred the honorary degree of *Master of Arts* in September, 1814, and the year before I had been elected a member of the Whig Society of the same college.

Columbia College, New York, in 1850, conferred on me the honorary degree of LL.D.

And in 1861, a like distinction was superadded by Harvard College, Massachusetts.

A cripple, unable to walk without assistance for three years, Scott, on retiring from all military duty,

October 31, 1861 — being broken down by recent official labors of from nine to seventeen hours a day, with a decided tendency to vertigo and dropsy, I had the honor to be waited on by President Lincoln, at the head of his Cabinet, who, in a neat and affecting address, took leave of the worn-out soldier.

Testimonials followed from several States, Governors, and Cities, the Legislature of New Jersey, Rahway, and Elizabeth ; two from Philadelphia — one headed by the Hon. Horace Binney, and the other by the Hon. Joseph R. Ingersoll—each signed by hundreds of the most substantial citizens. A similar compliment was received from St. Louis, very numerously signed. The City of New York, in no ordinary terms, heaped upon the retired soldier her distinguished approbation. The *Chamber of Commerce* and *The Union · Defence Committee*, each passed highly complimentary resolutions — the first presented by its venerable President, the late Peletiah Perit, at the head of a Committee, and the second by the eloquent Judge Edwards Pierrepont, on the part of the Committee of Defence, headed by Governor Hamilton Fish, Chairman.

I deeply regret the want of space for all of those

beautiful and honorable addresses, and it would be invidious to embody a part only.

In his first Annual Message to Congress (December, 1861), President Lincoln, prompted by his own kind and friendly nature, thus presented the autobiographer to the two Houses of Congress:

"Since your last adjournment, Lieutenant-General Scott has retired from the head of the army. During his long life the nation has not been unmindful of his merits; yet in calling to mind how faithfully and ably and brilliantly he has served his country, from a time far back in our history, when few now living had been born, and thenceforward continually — I cannot but think we are still his debtors. I submit, therefore, for your consideration what further mark of consideration is due to him and to ourselves as a grateful people."

THE END.

INDEX.

INDEX.

27*

9 783337 001513